Billy Wolf Bennett: He is a child of the plains, born to a mountaineer and his Cheyenne wife, growing up in a world of savage violence, ruthless nature, and blood fury. But there is a greater enemy that the young brave meets far from his homeland, when he journeys east to meet his Missouri kin. There he learns the hatred of people who judge him by the color of his skin, who see him as a half-breed heathen. And there he learns of tolerance—and vengeance.

Cleve Bennett: Yellow-Hair was a mountain man from the east who married into the Cheyenne, casting off his past life. A loving father, he knows he cannot protect Billy Wolf from danger forever. This fear is realized when his son is snagged in the Comanche battle for power—a war that rages endlessly and spills blood easily.

Second Son: The bravest and most skilled Cheyenne woman, she alone gives the victory cry that rings out when she fights for her son's life. But even the fierce warrior can feel heartache when her husband and her son make their journey east—and the pull of fear for their lives across the wide-open land.

MOUNTAIN MAJESTY

ASK YOUR BOOKSELLER
FOR THE BOOKS YOU HAVE MISSED

Mountain Majesty

=== BOOK FOUR ===

BLOOD
KIN

JOHN KILLDEER

BANTAM BOOKS

NEW YORK • TORONTO • LONDON • SYDNEY • AUCKLAND

BLOOD KIN
A Bantam Domain Book / March 1993

DOMAIN and the portrayal of a boxed "d" are trademarks
of Bantam Books,
a division of Bantam Doubleday Dell
Publishing Group, Inc.

The Mountain Majesty Series is the creation of Siegel & Siegel Ltd.

ISBN 0-553-28888-1

Published simultaneously in the United States and Canada

Bantam Books are published by Bantam Books, a division of Bantam
Doubleday Dell Publishing Group, Inc. Its trademark, consisting of the
words "Bantam Books" and the portrayal of a rooster, is Registered in
U.S. Patent and Trademark Office and in other countries. Marca Reg-
istrada. Bantam Books, 666 Fifth Avenue, New York, New York 10103.

PRINTED IN THE UNITED STATES OF AMERICA
RAD   0 9 8 7 6 5 4 3 2 1

chapter

— 1 —

The wind ruffled the cottonwood leaves, flapping them like tiny hands on their twisted stems. Billy Wolf, lying flat on his stomach beneath the largest of the trees edging the Cheyenne River, squinted across the plain to the west. Two horses moved there, heading away toward the northwest.

He pretended that he was one of those hunters, going out to find buffalo or mule deer. His small bow, fitted to his six-year-old size, lay beside him, and beyond it was a fat rabbit, skewered neatly through the neck. Billy Wolf already promised to become a hunter the equal of his warrior mother and his uncle Singing Wolf.

I

His father was not such a hunter. Though Cleve Bennett killed meat when it was needed, mainly he trapped the flat-tails in the mountains. All the boy's short life had been spent in the heights, helping his parents with their traps through the cold moons. He shivered, thinking of icy mornings when he handled the frozen bodies of beaver drowned when they were caught underwater.

Now it was summer, the time of ease and travel. Every spring they had taken the bales of skins, trapped and treated over the cold season, and gone down from the heights to the Rendezvous, wherever it was being held that year. When he was only a tiny child, he had seen Bear Lake, lying like a piece of displaced sky under the dry hills to the east of it. He could still feel the surge of delight he had felt at seeing that great expanse of water, cold and sweet and blue.

Last year the Rendezvous had been very close to the Absaroka country where his people best liked to trap, and this year it had been on the Popo Agie River, not far from that earlier gathering. That had left them plenty of time to visit new country, but instead Cleve and Second Son decided to take Billy Wolf back east to see his Cheyenne kindred.

It was the first time he had seen the great prairieland, which swept eastward from the backbone of the mountains, so vast and so empty that it was almost frightening. Billy Wolf had felt that without the mountains pinning him onto the surface of this endless plain, he might fall upward into the sky and float away like an eagle or a hawk.

They had crossed rivers, plunged through seas of buffalo grass that tickled their knees as they rode, coming at last to a tall rock, where Second Son, his mother, built a fire that sent a plume of smoke into the windswept sky. Her signaling puffs were carried away quickly on the rampageous wind, but within two days a rider came into view.

Billy Wolf grinned, thinking of his uncle, who had read that faint signal with the eyes of his spirit and come as fast as his horse could travel. Singing Wolf was unlike anyone. Tall and slender, his eyes still and calm, his feathers precisely arranged in the braids down the front of his hair, and his moccasins beautifully beaded, he was more impressive than any of the French *coureurs de bois* or American mountain men the boy had met before. This was a man who knew his mind. That was the impression the child had before any other, and he had not changed his thinking.

The village had been a revelation, too. The tipis, though shaped like the one in which his own family lived when not traveling, were decorated with painted animals and men, hunting, fighting, dancing. Dogs sniffed and snarled everywhere, and Billy Wolf fell in love at once with a yellow pup. His mother's nephew, who owned the pup's mother, gave it to him at once, and Cleve seemed pleased to have a dog in the family again.

That made Billy Wolf think of Snip. He had been very young when his father's old dog died saving him and his mother from an enemy. He couldn't remember him at all, though he felt that he could because of the tales his father and mother told over the fire at night. Snip had been a friend, and this new pup was going to be one, too, so the boy named him Snip, hoping that one day he would equal the dog that had been his father's.

As if the thought conjured him up, there came the patter of awkward paws, the sound of earnest panting, and a hairy yellow face peered out of the reeds. The boy held out a hand, and already being trained according to Cleve's instructions, the pup came quietly to his side and laid his damp chin in Billy Wolf's palm.

The other boys marveled at that, for the Tsistsistas used dogs as haulers of burdens or as meat, but they had never trained them in the ways that Cleve Bennett knew. Having an animal that came and went when signaled with a whistle and that sat in place, unstirring, until freed to move was a thing that amazed them. When Snip learned to fetch a thrown stick, every boy in camp claimed some scruffy pup and began training him to do the same.

Billy Wolf rose and clicked his fingers. The pup came to his heels and followed silently. The boy returned quietly along the path leading toward the tipi his family had raised when they came home to the Burning Heart band, his mother's own people.

There was a warm spot in Billy Wolf's heart. He had never wanted for comfort. His parents cared for him without a lot of talk but with constant attention. Still, the dog filled a gap in his young spirit that he hadn't known was there until it was filled.

This summer had filled a lot of gaps, in fact. He had a grandfather, very old and so wrinkled that his face was like a hillside scarred by rain and wind. The old man sat and talked with him often, as if treasuring this time with his grandson, which might not come again. Young as he was, Billy Wolf felt the same.

He had an uncle who was so majestic, so wise, so kind that the boy was shy about approaching him. He also had a friend—not a boy, but the nephew of his mother.

Cub had shed his childish name and was now Rakes the Sky with Lightning, a warrior, though still a very young one. It was rare that such a youngster, full of the excitement of occasional raids on Pawnee or Comanche ponies, would take the trouble to befriend a child.

To have a Kit Fox warrior, even one still a novice, as a friend, elevated Billy Wolf in the regard of those youngsters who might have regarded this pale-haired stranger as something of an outcast. When Cleve told him that this same Lightning, then called Cub, had taught him to use the bow and the lance, the boy's satisfaction was complete.

He paused from time to time to peer between cottonwoods and willows at the distant horsemen. Lightning and his good friend Buffalo Wallow were disappearing over the swell of the ground and soon were no longer visible to his longing gaze. Sometimes he felt sad that he was still only a small boy and could not go out on a raid or a hunt with the men.

Snip nudged his ankle with a cold nose. The fluff at the end of his yellow tail waggled. Billy Wolf grinned. Though his father and mother took him with them everywhere, hunting and trapping and scouting for enemies, they were so tall and wise and powerful that they intimidated him a bit.

Now he had a friend even smaller than he was, who would go with them when they left the Burning Hearts. He put a bare foot on the dog's back and wiggled his toes in the pale fur. Snip lay down, rolled onto his side, and grunted with ecstasy as his small master tickled and patted him.

The morning was clear, the wind clean and brisk out of the northwest. Billy Wolf straightened and rubbed his stomach. He would go home to the tipi and see if there was meat left from the night before. His lean belly seemed always empty, and he knew his mother, unlike more ordinary ones, never begrudged his eating what he wanted.

He came up out of the river's edge, over the roll of ground beyond which only occasional scrub grew, and saw the random pattern of the camp lying across a shallow valley through which a creek fed into the larger stream. Women worked over hides staked out in circles on the ground between the shelters. Children too small to go fishing or hunting or gathering ran about with tiny bows or sat with stick and leather dolls in the shade of the tipis.

It was a busy scene, and Billy Wolf absorbed it into his mind. It must last for a long time, he knew, for his mother had explained to him that they had come to visit, not to stay. Soon he would go eastward with his father, to that unimaginable place from which Yellow Hair had come.

Missouri. It had an alien ring to it.

He hadn't quite understood why it was that Second Son was not to come with them, and his father looked so odd when he asked that he soon gave it up. Still, he felt a strangeness about that journey, and he could only think that the pale-skinned trapper they had met beside the Popo Agie had brought news of the family Cleve Bennett left back in the country from which he had come, long before his son was born.

As he trudged down the long slope toward the tipi at the edge of the encampment, the boy felt something in the air, growing stronger. A vibration rumbled beneath his tough bare soles, and he rose to his full height and stared about to find what might be coming. Then he gave a shrill yell and ran with all his might toward the busy women.

"*Shi shinni wo is tan iu!*" he shouted, pounding toward the nearest group.

The women knew that name too well, for those the white men called Comanche often raided their camps for horses. The fierce warriors ranged far northward in summer after buffalo and plunder, and many of the Tsistsistas had lost their horses and their lives to those depredations.

Head down, fists pistoning, the boy sped toward what safety there might be in a camp empty of his father and mother. Both had gone today with his uncle Singing Wolf on some errand to the north.

Ahead, a woman called a warning, and he turned enough to see that the pounding was not only caused by the thunder of his heart. A great red horse bore down on him, its rider's face, striped in red and black, a terrifying mask whose gaze was fixed upon him.

"Aieee!" shrieked Billy Wolf as the Comanche swooped.

An iron arm hooked around his waist as the warrior leaned out and down, then swung up again with the wriggling boy laid across the horse's shoulder. The animal's coarse hair, sticky with sweat, was hot under Billy Wolf's belly and chest, and the movement of the bones of the shoulders dug into him.

Grass flowed away dizzily as the boy gasped for breath and opened his eyes. He twisted his head, to see the tipis now very near. A stocky figure stepped from behind one of the lodges, loosed an arrow, reloaded, and loosed another.

The warrior grunted, and the boy hoped fiercely that one of the arrows had struck him. Something hot began seeping onto Billy Wolf's side, and the hard hand holding him in place loosed its grip very slightly. The boy tensed, bent backward like a bow, and flung himself off the galloping horse.

He landed hard, knocking his breath out, and for a moment he lay flat, ignoring the deadly hooves that pounded on all sides as the other Comanche dashed past. None struck him, and when at last he was able to fill his lungs, the raid had moved on into the village. Only Snip was there, whimpering and licking his face as if the dog knew what a terrible thing had almost happened.

Billy Wolf sat up and shook the hair and dust out of his eyes. Dead grass clung to his skin as he rose shakily to his feet and stared toward the flurry of action taking place around the camp. More women and old men and youngsters had armed themselves, and arrows were flying fast.

At least two of the Comanche were down, but a double handful more were yipping around the loose curve of lodges while at least twenty more were driving away the herd that had been pastured on the rolling grassland beyond the village. Fury rose into the boy's throat, making his head throb with painful anger.

His small bow had been dropped, with the rabbit, far back where he was captured, but he found a palm-sized rock, took it up, and ran toward the fray, yelling at the top of his lungs. No one was aware of him until he was close enough to clip a wheeling Comanche pony on the ear. It snorted, twisting aside, and threw the warrior who rode it.

A horse swerved beneath the knees of its rider and headed toward Billy Wolf, the youth astride it leaning far out, his black eyes blazing with purpose. The boy turned and ran, but the hooves thundered after him, coming closer and closer. Snip, running ahead, turned back and began to bark, but that didn't stop the oncoming warrior.

Again Billy Wolf was scooped up into steely arms and this time something hit his head with stunning impact. He tried to shout, to struggle, but blackness oozed over him, and he went out completely.

chapter

— 2 —

The wind was warm and dry, gusting across the buffalo grass, making it ripple in long undulations. Rakes the Sky with Lightning kicked his heels into his pony's flanks. The sorrel gelding, stolen from the Comanche last fall on a raid southward, trotted forward amid a rattle of insects.

Beside him, Buffalo Wallow's mare rustled the tall growth, and Lightning felt his friend's presence as a warmth at his side. It was a fine day to hunt. A fine day to be alive, in fact, and the young warrior rose to his knees on the back of his gelding and let out a long yip, just from high spirits.

In the distance there came a shrill warble in reply. He halted the horse and listened.

Buffalo said, "That is your father's cry. Do they return so soon?"

Lightning shook his head. With the suddenness that had given him the name Lightning, he had a flash of intuition; the day darkened about him, though the sun still shone and the wind was sweet with grass. Something was wrong. He sometimes had these dark premonitions, and he had learned to heed them.

He turned to Buffalo Wallow and gestured toward the source of the call. "Ride fast to meet them. Tell them that I return to the village. There is trouble there. I feel it in the wind!" He kicked his sorrel with both heels, and the gelding took off at a gallop, heading back toward the fringe of trees marking the river.

He knew that Buffalo would do as he was bidden, for the boy had followed his lead since they were children. His friend was faithful, brave, strong, and not very bright. Sometimes Lightning felt as if he had, in this young man, an extra body, to use as he needed it.

The gelding was lathered and panting deeply by the time they reached the edge of the valley sheltering the Burning Heart camp. Fury rose into Lightning's throat as he saw smoke from scattered fires blowing across a scene of utmost confusion. Tipis lay flat or slanted drunkenly. Dark blots that he knew to be bodies lay as if abandoned. A few moving shapes beat at fires with smoking robes or dragged wounded away from danger.

With a whoop of rage, the young warrior raised his lance and urged his gelding down the slope toward the distant line of raiders, who were already retreating southward. Making a quick judgment—Lightning was a fitting name for more than one reason—he turned and raced toward the camp. There he dropped from his horse to see to a woman who was trying to rise despite the lance that pinned her leg to the ground.

"Stop," he said to her, removing the lance with a swift jerk. "You will bleed too much if you move. Stay there, Little Turtle. I will help you when I see to the others."

The words were braver than he felt. Suddenly the young warrior realized how grave this situation must be, for he saw no young men among those now gathering around the wounded and the dead. They had gone about their usual business on this summer morning when nothing seemed to threaten.

Now they were too far away to arrive quickly, even if they could hear the cries and whinnies of the battle. The women and the old men had fought off this raid.

"My grandfather!" Lightning yelled to his mother, who was lifting a crying child. "Is he all right?"

The tipi the old man shared with Singing Wolf's family teetered as if about to fall flat, as the one next to it had already done. "He was inside. I was out. I have not seen him, my son. Go to him!" Nesting Bird cried.

Lightning found the old man struggling beneath a heavy buffalo robe that had fallen onto him from the spot where it hung, when the tipi was upset. It took him only a moment to free his grandfather.

The ancient face was taut with anger as he crawled out at last and stood shakily before the tipi. "Grandson, I saw Second Son's boy, just before the Shinni came. He was at the edge of the river, starting toward me, and I went back and sat, waiting for him. It was his voice that gave the warning. But I do not see him. My eyes are old. Use your young ones to look over those who are here. I have a terrible premonition that he has been taken."

Lightning helped him to sit and turned to go through the count of the wounded and the well, searching for his warrior-aunt's child. There was no sign of Billy Wolf, though a woman remembered seeing him caught up by one of the attacking Comanche.

"That one is brave," she said. "He threw a stone and hit the horse of one of the warriors. The man fell, but another came riding and swept up the child. They rode away after the other raiders, going south."

Lightning turned and ran toward his gelding, intending to ride after the retreating Comanche, but his grandfather, bent and feeble as he was, waited beside the horse. "Do not go alone. It is brave but foolish, and we need all our young warriors. I have heard the cry that tells me your father and the boy's parents come soon. Wait for them, Rakes the Sky with Lightning. That is the part of wisdom."

There came a quavering yell to the northwest, and distant specks swam into view over the roll of land rising there. With a feeling of relief, Lightning realized that Singing Wolf would soon be with him. His father knew their enemy with the accuracy that only a peace chief, dedicated to keeping the tribes from conflict if possible, could possess.

Billy Wolf was dizzy, sick at his stomach from hanging upside down over the shoulders of the Comanche pony. The ground spun away in a blur beneath him, and he learned to keep his eyes closed. If he pretended to be unconscious, he thought, perhaps he could surprise the man whose iron hand still held him clamped onto the horse. Escape was always possible. His mother and his father had taught him that all his life.

But that hand never loosed its grip, and at last the bouncing under his belly made the boy retch and vomit a stream of bitterness into the wind of their passing. Then his captor lifted him with one effortless gesture and set him before him, holding him fast.

The prairie rolled away beneath the horse's hooves, every moment putting more distance between the child and everything familiar. Others were abducted and raised as members of the raiders' tribes, he knew. There were those in the Tsistsistas camp who had been born in the villages of Sioux and Blackfoot, Pawnee and Comanche. They seemed never to question their status as members of the tribe.

The thought chilled him. Would he forget, if he could not escape? How could he ever lose the memory of his tall father, golden-haired, strong, and swift of foot? How could he forget his mother, who was a man and a warrior to all her people?

Surely someone would come after them! He had seen his grandfather standing before his tipi as he approached the village. The old man might be weakened by age, but his eye and his ear were still alert, if no longer sharp. He would know what happened. He would send someone after his grandson!

But for now there was nothing to do but cling to the whipping mane, decorated with feathers for this raid, and hope his captor wouldn't squeeze him in half. Billy Wolf was unfamiliar with this part of the plains country, and every swell, every rock, every stretch of neck-high grass looked just like all the rest.

The sun moved on its normal way, however, and the child kept watch on its progression up the sky. He knew south and north, east and west; if he could escape and run north again, he would eventually come to the river, which flowed across the wide lands to meet that Great River of which his father had told him. He could travel up and down the stream until he came to the camp of his people.

When the raiding party slowed to rest the horses, the young warrior who had taken him tied his hands cruelly tight with thongs and looped his feet together beneath the barrel of the horse they rode. Secured so, Billy Wolf could not even get down to pee, and to his shame he wet himself and the horse equally while the raiders laughed at his discomfort.

That filled the boy with fury. They might have let him relieve himself, as they had done openly, without risk of his running away. A resolve was growing in him to run at the first opportunity, no matter if it meant going alone across the plain, without food or mount, without weapon or even moccasins to keep his feet from becoming too sore to walk. If he died of it, then at least he would be free of these rude young men.

They mounted again, driving the stolen horses slowly now, letting them rest. Billy Wolf knew the Shinni thought themselves safe, so far from the village they had raided. He almost laughed aloud, thinking of Cleve's anger and Second Son's skill and ferocity joined in pursuit of their son.

And his uncle would come with them, the boy thought. Rakes the Sky with Lightning and Buffalo Wallow and many of the young warriors who stood in awe of his mother and his uncle would ride to find him.

The other boys among the Burning Hearts would be aflame with envy. If, of course, he ever returned to crow to them about his escapade.

The sun topped the sky and started down again. The sea of grass, now tan with summer heat, waved endlessly before and behind and on either side of them. On the edge of the sky, Billy Wolf began to see something—a shadow line that became more distinct as they traveled. Trees along a stream, he thought. He had seen many as they journeyed from the mountains toward the lands of his mother's people.

When they stopped at last, it was at the bend of a stream bed, almost dry at this time of year. Cottonwoods showed that water lay not too far beneath the soil, and that was proved by the trickle of water at the bottom of the shallow arroyo. The boy could hear the faint sound of the ripples against rocks as he was lifted down from the horse and dropped roughly onto the ground.

His hands were asleep, his feet numb. If he had been alone, it would have been impossible for him to run, or even to stand. But the loosing of his bonds allowed a prickle of feeling to return to his limbs, which soon were burning as if held in the midst of a fire.

Tears filled his eyes, but he didn't let them fall. The boy endured the pain without whimpering until he was able to clench his fists and feel his fingers, wiggle his feet and curl his toes. When the warrior jerked him upright and cut loose the thongs, he pretended to stagger, still numbed by being tied. Tonight he would escape, if that was possible.

They flung him scraps of jerky from their pouches. One

dropped an almost empty waterskin beside him, and he
drank the last drops thirstily, knowing that if he managed
to get away, he would find the lack of water worse than
anything else. Even with the training his mother had given
him in managing thirst, he knew it was going to be very
hard.

The raiders watered their horses, mounted again, and
rode some distance before pausing for the night. A clever
warrior did not camp too near water, for both predators
and enemies tended to seek out water holes and streams.
Billy Wolf dropped off to sleep the instant his captor
dropped him into a thick growth of grass, and he knew
nothing for a long while.

He woke gazing into the clear eye of a full moon. Without stirring, the child rolled his gaze around the area
within range, checking out the long lumps that were the
raiding party, the tall grass walling in the camp. He could
see the shape of a horse's head and ears thrust against the
sky at some distance beyond the trampled patch where
the men slept.

He could hear the occasional snuffles and stamps of the
animals, but he heard no sound from the man who must
be on watch over the sleeping group. That warrior knew
his enemies might come quickly on the trail, and he took
no chances.

Billy Wolf sighed and turned, as if still asleep. The nearest sleeper—his captor, he felt certain—did not stir. The
boy worked one arm above his head, slowly, silently, finding space between the heavy grass stalks. His feet were tied
again, but they had left his hands free, and he managed to
slither blindly into the grass until his entire body was hidden.

Only then did he sit and loose the ties around his ankles. Then he looked up. A man's head would thrust above the level of the grass tops, but he could walk upright once he worked clear of the watcher, wherever he might be. Sometimes it was handy to be a child, though almost always it made everything very hard.

He lay flat again, working his way northward, guiding himself by frequent glimpses of the moon, which was still in the east. He had to detour around the area where the horses grazed, taking care not to alarm them. Nothing waked a Comanche as quickly as an unusual sound among his horses, the boy had heard his grandfather say.

The moon had moved across the sky above him and was in the west by the time Billy Wolf felt himself clear of the raiders and dared to rise. Running was out of the question.

Even horses had a hard time running in the high grass, which was now dried with summer and drought, the edges of the blades sharp enough to slice his skin if he moved too quickly through the tall growth. Had he tried to go fast, he would have been sliced to ribbons.

His eyes heavy, his legs growing more and more weary, the boy plodded along, developing a rhythm for sweeping aside the grass stalks with both arms, stepping, sweeping again, stepping again, until he was almost walking in his sleep. He woke fully when he looked for the moon and found himself walking toward it, now in the west, instead of north toward the village of his people.

That frightened him, for he could walk forever, or until he fell dead, and never find anything helpful if he went westward. The mountains that he had known as home were too far to be reached by his short legs, even if he had water and food in plenty.

That reminded him that he'd tucked the remnant of the jerky under the waist string of his loincloth, and he dug for it. To his relief, it was still there, and he chewed it slowly, letting saliva form, swallowing deliberately. He took only a nibble, for it would make him thirsty, and he had seen no sign of water nearer than the river. That was guarded too well by the Comanche who had taken him.

Leg up, step, sweep, leg up, step, sweep—now he kept his wits about him, moving at a snaillike pace toward the north.

If those behind him didn't miss him too soon, and if they couldn't find his insignificant trail amid those of mule deer and jackrabbits and stray buffalo that meandered through the grass, he might come, at last, to his grandfather's tipi and find safety again.

chapter

— 3 —

It had been a satisfying journey, Cleve thought. Riding his old horse Socks across the rolling flatlands, amid the sweet smells of grass drying in the sun, midsummer blossoms, and the clean air itself, was enough to set a man up right. Being in the company of his wife and his brother-in-law made it even better.

They'd accomplished a lot, too. As a peace chief, Singing Wolf had been busy keeping the Burning Hearts' young men content with hunting and tending the horses for just about as long as anyone could hope to. Those hot-blooded youngsters of the Kit Foxes, the Dog Soldiers, and the Red Shields were hot for raiding, though the nearest considerable herd belonged to the Arapaho, who were the Tsistsistas' traditional allies.

As they jogged along through the high grass Cleve was listening to the low-voiced conversation between Second Son and her brother. "It is the time when Comanche turn northward," she was saying. "You were wise to talk with the Arapaho. If any of their horses are stolen by our young warriors, it is best to agree to send them back in the hands of the shamefaced young men who took them. We will need allies once the summer raids begin."

Even now, after so many years of living in the Cheyenne way, Cleve found it hard to accept the fact that stealing horses was, among the plains people, a sort of game. Lives were lost, of course, but not many. He could recall times when the bare-knuckle fights that entertained his fellow Missourians had ended in death, and nobody thought anything much about it.

It was the idea of stealing for sport that was hard for him to deal with. He had learned, in his time with Second Son, that property meant nothing to her. That attitude extended to those of her people whom he had met. Honor, courage, the regard of peers—these were what they coveted.

Without hesitation, Second Son would give a winter's harvest of plews to one she decided needed it. He had almost come to harsh words with her over that, the spring she had donated a horseload of furs to Old Joe Ferris, who had been their closest friend since their first Rendezvous, six years ago. Ferris had the worst luck of anybody, and that year had been no different.

She had looked into his eyes, her dark gaze sparking.

"He was caught in a flood. He lost most of his horses and most of his skins. Do we allow a friend to suffer when we have more furs and more horses than we need?"

She was right, of course. They had been fortunate in their trapping every winter since their first one together, and the horses they possessed after the death of his first partner had multiplied, for there had been several mares among them. Second Son's stallion, captured years before in a horse raid on the Pawnee, had proven himself many times over, and his colts were sound ones.

They had more horses than they needed, and once Cleve cooled down, he realized that he should have offered Ferris their extras without prompting. His early training, which taught him greed for possessions, now hampered him in his dealings with the Indians, and the older he got the more he understood that.

Cleve grinned as he rode, thinking of his stash of gold coin. Greed or not, white men needed money at times, and he never intended to be lacking if that time came. A percentage of his plews, every summer, was turned into gold. If he never needed it, his son might. Being a half blood would be much easier if he had coin in hand. White men would respect Satan himself if he came with a full purse, as the trapper knew all too well.

He was too wise to carry his hoard or to confide its location to anyone except his wife. But Cleve knew that few would search a bear's den, particularly one that showed no sign of the presence of man. In summer it was a cramped space littered with debris, and in winter its lawful tenant was asleep on top of the gold, which was buried beneath the beast's resting place. On his last visit, when he unearthed a gift for his kin in Missouri, it had been hard even for him to find his hoard.

Second Son's horse shied at something in the grass, and she controlled it effortlessly. Cleve glanced aside at the young mare she rode, remembering Shadow, the old mare his wife had loved so well. That horse had died after the birth of her last foal, but the little filly had lived, and now as a feisty two-year-old, young Shadow looked well able to fill her dam's place. She already showed a convenient turn of speed.

Singing Wolf rode up on the other side of Socks, but he did not glance at Cleve. He was looking south and east, toward the camp of the band. His face was still, and his eyes creased deeply at the corners, as if were trying to see beyond the horizon.

Cleve knew the man well by now, and when Singing Wolf looked like that, it was time to count your arrows and string your bow. "What is it?" he asked, when the sharp gaze returned from the edge of the sky.

"Something . . . we must ride quickly to the camp." Singing Wolf raised his head and sent a shrill cry into the sky, and from a distance there came an answer.

Cleve kicked Socks sharply in the sides, and the gelding quickened his pace to keep up with the other pair of horses. The three sped through the tall grass until they reached a wide swath trampled by a roaming herd of buffalo; that gave them faster footing, and they galloped toward the river and the village. Before they had gone far, another rider appeared, off to one side but angling to intercept them.

"Buffalo Wallow," said Second Son. "Without Cub—I mean Lightning."

They did not pause when the young man joined them, for they were already filled with apprehension. Something was happening among the band, and Singing Wolf's son had, in his usual swift fashion, felt it and turned back to help his people. They needed no word from Buffalo Wallow to tell them as much.

Now Cleve felt a tension in his own gut. His son was there with the rest of the band, and though the People were tough and always ready to defend their camp, a six-year-old was so small and so vulnerable. The thought of his son in danger sent Cleve pelting ahead, even though his mount was much older than the other two.

He could see smoke—more than should rise from the small and controlled fires before the lodges. This was dark and straggled across the sky on the wind that always swept the plains. As the line of cottonwoods along the river came into view, Cleve noted that tipis were down; some were burning, and dark figures moved about them in disciplined haste. There had been casualties.

The four riders now were side by side, urging their mounts forward, their lances held ready in case any attacker lingered about the village. But nobody appeared, and the horse herd that had grazed on the slope of a swell behind the camp was gone, except for scattered animals that had escaped the sweep of the raiders.

The tipi that Singing Wolf and his wives shared with their children and his father, Buffalo Horn, was almost down, lying drunkenly on broken lodgepoles. The old man sat before the misshapen door hole, his lined face drawn with worry.

As the riders dropped from their horses before him Buffalo Horn raised his hands. "They have come, the Shinni, and taken my grandson. Go quickly! Go quickly and find him! We have looked everywhere, but only his dog can we find."

Cleve looked about and saw the yellow pup his son called Snip sitting beyond the old man, its tongue lolling, its big eyes anxious. If this had been the old Snip, friend and companion for so many years, the dog would have trailed his small master no matter how far the Comanche had taken him.

But this pup was too young . . . or was he? His legs were short, but if carried before a rider, could he, perhaps, scent Billy Wolf and guide those who pursued his captors? It was worth trying, and the animal was too small to put any extra burden on a horse.

Second Son, as if reading his mind, nodded, and Cleve scooped up the dog and was back on Socks before his wife was well mounted. They turned together and set off at a ground-eating pace gauged to get the most out of their horses. There was no time to catch fresh ones, already spooked by the raid, and these tired animals would have to endure.

Socks fell behind Shadow, letting the young mare's gait set his own. Into the south Cleve followed Second Son, his teeth grinding with rage, his heart heavy with worry. What Second Son felt he could not tell from her look, but he knew her too well to doubt that she also was filled with fury and concern. He would hate to be the Comanche upon whom her wrath must fall.

Buffalo Wallow had remained behind with the band to help with the wounded. Ahead, somewhere, rode Rakes the Sky with Lightning, and Cleve had great confidence that the young man's instinct would guide him well. He would know not to alarm the Comanche as he tracked his young kinsman.

Yet trusting his son's life to someone so young was not a comfortable thing, and Cleve begrudged the times when they walked the horses to give them rest. But the sign was clear and the droppings they passed were still soft. They would find the Comanche tonight, he felt certain, while they were camped.

He only hoped that Billy Wolf kept his wits and made no problem for the raiders. They had been known to knock troublesome children on the head.

The sun set, leaving the plain in shades of black and gray until the moon rose, full and round on the eastern horizon. Then everything was edged with silver, and the shapes of the other riders were sharp and yet somehow ghostly. Cleve shivered as he kicked Socks into motion, following Singing Wolf's paint mare that once again was headed toward the south.

Now a dark line, uneven against the pale sky, showed where a stream ran across the prairie toward the distant river. They had been riding slowly for the past half hour, the hooves of their mounts cushioned by the thick, drying grass. Now, as one, the three riders halted, for if the Comanche paused for the night, it would be near water, though not too close.

The horses would remain here, far enough so that their footfalls as they grazed could not sound ahead through the ground to warn the Shinni that vengeance was upon them. What must be done now must be accomplished by those on foot.

Already Second Son had armed herself, her bow slung

over her back, her knife near at hand. Singing Wolf was chanting softly, his voice inaudible from more than a few feet away. It was not the way of his people to attack at night, but this was his nephew who was in danger.

Cleve was ready. He moved forward through the head-high grass, his back bent enough to hide his shining hair as he picked his way toward the distant creek. From time to time he paused to listen, and when the chitter of a night bird quivered through the air, he knew it to come from human lips. Second Son had taught him well.

Behind him he heard nothing, for his wife and her brother were skilled at stalking without being heard. That signal had not concerned them, for it was too far ahead. But something had disturbed the camp, that was clear. Another voice trilled a coyote's cry into the night sky. Again, this was a man, not an animal.

Cleve made a motion with his hand, and even in the dim thicknesses of grass his companions understood. They came close and, heads together, consulted.

"Has Lightning been rash and warned them of his presence?" asked the warrior's father. "That would not be like him."

"I think not," said Second Son. "That is not a warning but a signal between searchers. Yellow Hair, our son has escaped. If I were a white man, I would make a bet on that."

Cleve nodded in the dimness, feeling sure she was right. Ever since he could walk, Billy Wolf had been reared to behave like a man. No mountain child enjoyed a time of foolishness like that allowed to white children in settled country. Alertness, cool wits, the ability to move silently and to endure terror without whimpering were the things required for survival in the harsh lands where Billy Wolf had grown up.

Cleve glanced about at the almost indistinguishable faces of his wife and her brother. Then, as one, they sank to their bellies in the grass and slithered toward the place from which those signals had come.

It seemed a very long way. Hands and knees became painful, and low-lying grass blades left networks of tiny cuts on Cleve's neck and wrists as he moved through the growth. He hardly noticed, so concentrated was he upon reaching that stream.

The Comanche would be camped beyond it, on high ground and yet in cover. That was their way, he knew, and he intended to approach their position from a direction they did not expect. Second Son would have her own plan, as would Singing Wolf. He was learning the Indian way, each man creating his own tactics as a conflict developed, each depending upon the others to do the same without planning ahead.

From very near there came a rustle. It was deliberate; no one concealed in the grass would risk an accidental one. Cleve pursed his lips and quavered a sleepy birdcall— once, twice, pause, once.

"*Sssss,*" came the reply, almost too soft to hear.

It was Lightning. Who else would be lying hidden in the grass while the Comanche signaled their loss through the night? When Cleve had moved another few rods through the tall growth, he saw a pair of bright eyes in a shaft of moonlight.

"You have come at last," said his wife's nephew. "It took you very long, but it is better to come late than not to come at all. The boy was among those camped beyond the stream. They are now searching through the grass and down the ravine, so I can only think he has managed to get away from them. What do we do now?"

That was a good question. If it had been a matter of swooping down on the camp, locating and taking away the boy and leaving his captors in disarray, that would have been one thing. Now they had a plain full of disturbed Comanche, a child who was out there somewhere, free but unprotected, and four people who had to do something quickly.

"I will attack the camp beyond the stream," said Singing Wolf. "That will distract them from their hunt."

Cleve nodded. That was a sensible move, which should not endanger Billy Wolf.

"I will range this side of the stream, searching through the grass. If I meet any of the Shinni, they will regret it very much." That was Second Son, and Cleve knew that her words were entirely accurate.

"Lightning and I, if he is willing, will go down into the ravine and move upstream toward the sounds of movement. If anyone finds the boy, he must cross the ravine to take him back to camp. If those who are moved by your attack come to join their brothers in the grass, they must cross as well," said Cleve.

"We will deal with anyone who comes our way, and if the boy is hiding, upstream or down, we will find him. It is the best plan that I can think of." Cleve looked about and saw agreement on the faces of the others.

"I will go out first, cross the ravine downstream, and attack them from the south," said his brother-in-law. "They will not expect attack from there, I think. Give me until the moon is just there." He raised his hand to indicate the patch of sky to which the moon must move before they began their own part of the campaign.

"I will move out very quietly, very slowly, and comb the grass between this point and the stream," said Second Son. "I will call like a hunting owl if I find our son." Her gaze was warm, even in the tenuous light.

"And I will go with Lightning to the east and into the ravine downstream. I will wait until I hear a coyote cry— and I hope he will do that more convincingly than the one we heard earlier."

The departure of the four was so quiet that a jackrabbit crouching in a clump of grass within a stone's throw of them did not interrupt his nightly meal. Cleve and Lightning slithered along on their bellies now, propelling themselves with elbows and toes so as to make the least possible disturbance in the grass.

It was a very long half mile, but at last they reached the edge of the gully, which was an abrupt cut in the plain. Its dark depths glittered with reflected moonlight off faces of rock and the slim trickle of water at its bottom. Cleve listened hard, but he could hear only those calls from the searching Comanche, now some distance to the west. The ravine was quiet, except for the sound of moving water.

He slid, silent as a serpent, over the edge and found purchase among the layers of rock and soil the stream had cut. Behind him Lightning waited, and only when he was safely down and in the cover of shadow did the young man descend to join him.

Together, wary and watchful, they started to move up the stream, their steps inaudible as they slid their feet along the bottom. If the journey through the grass had seemed long, this was endless.

chapter

— 4 —

Cold fury filled Second Son as she slid away into the grass with Snip secured in a sort of sling behind her back. She took pride in the fact that she hardly disturbed the tall growth as she slipped between clumps of root, though small animals scuttered away before her: mice and small snakes, ferrets and rabbits moved out of her path, without noise or panic.

A bird rose with a rush of wings, and she froze, hoping that no Shinni was near enough to note its panic-stricken flight. The pup, as if knowing the need for silence, didn't even whimper.

There was no twitter or animal cry that might be a Comanche warning. After a moment she moved again, keeping the moon's slanting light through the grass stalks in focus so that she would not miss her direction. When she rose to her feet at last, peering between the tops of the grasses, she saw that she was dead on target.

The dark line of trees loomed near at hand along the creekbank. As she watched, the grass shivered some yards beyond her, and a dark head shone briefly in the moonlight. The Shinni were here, as well as farther out on the plain.

She must remove a few in order to make it easier to conduct her own search. It would be just as well to begin with this one, near at hand and unsuspecting. She eased the confined pup to the ground, put a warning hand on his head, and watched her prey.

She noted his direction as he moved out of the tall grass to stand on the bank of the stream, staring down into its dark rift. Second Son crept to the edge of the thick growth and ran silently across the space between them, her body striking that of her prey and knocking him into a leaning cottonwood.

It took the wind out of him, so he couldn't cry out, but he managed to grapple strongly as she came in with her knife. He was larger than she but not much stronger; Second Son knew every dirty trick ever invented and had originated more than a few of her own. One leg hooked behind his; her shoulder went into his belly, and she raised her head sharply, butting him beneath his chin as hard as she could.

His head struck the cottonwood with a dull *thunk*. Before he could regain his wits, she had cut his throat and dragged him into the grass, pulling bent stalks back into place to conceal his body. Dark blood shone faintly in the moonlight, black smears on the gray grass. When she passed with the dog again on her back, the pup whimpered deep in his throat but made no real noise.

Second Son knew that Yellow Hair and her nephew would find Billy Wolf if he were in the stream. She turned way from the bank and melted back into the grass. The moon was halfway down in the west now, and from the occasional chirps or howls from the Comanche she knew they were casting about blindly, without a trail to guide them.

It had to be her son they were seeking. He was clever, that one, and escaping would be no trick for him. Surviving on the plain, without help, was another matter entirely.

She listened hard, standing like another stalk amid the billows of that grassy sea. Ahead and to her left she heard an irritable quaver, this one real . . . a bird disturbed by some incautious passerby. That gave her direction and she turned, angling toward the sound, keeping her bearings by glancing up from time to time to find a certain patch of stars.

She came face-to-face with the next Shinni without warning. He had been listening hard for any sound amid the grass, but she moved so quietly that he had not heard her approach. Then she was looking into his startled eyes.

This was no raw youngster. He had his knife in his hand, and he came at her in a rush made more dangerous by his bulk, for he was even bigger than the last Comanche. Second Son dropped an instant before he reached her and rolled against his legs, bringing him down. His mouth opened to shout a warning to his companions, even as he turned like a snake to strike her with his blade. Her own hand, holding the fine steel knife for which Cleve had

traded, moved more quickly than her victim could antici-
pate.

He gurgled as it penetrated below his throat, slipping
sideways beneath the rib below his collarbone. Then she
struck with the inferior blade in her left hand, serpent
quick, at his Adam's apple to stop the cry he was trying to
utter.

He caught her around the waist with arms that were in-
credibly strong, even at the edge of death. His blood was
hot on her body, running down in sticky streams as she
rolled aside, trying to protect the pup on her back but still
clasped in that iron grip. She kicked frantically at his leg,
while driving the knives deeper into him.

His teeth sank into her breast, but now she felt the arms
losing their power as blood streamed out of her opponent.
She brought down both elbows on the arms around her,
pushing him away with her knees at the same time. With
a last gargling gasp, the warrior rolled away and his glaz-
ing eyes glinted in the moonlight.

Still stinking of his blood, Second Son rose and listened,
waiting for some indication of any other presence. The
pup was whining softly. A coyote wailed beyond the
stream. A hunting owl moved across the moon, the whisper of its wings almost inaudible. An irritated chirrup
came from one of the Shinni, but he was well off to the
east and she ignored him.

Second Son reached to unsling the pup and set him on
his feet. He looked up at her, his eyes shining green in the
moonlight, his skimpy tail wagging questioningly. She set
him down on the grass beyond the high growth and moved
parallel to the creek, the dog following her obediently.

Suddenly his ears pricked up and he stopped to sniff the

ground. His tail wagged furiously as he looked up, then down, then up again. She left the shelter of the grass and knelt beside him, but there was no visible sign on the ground.

Without waiting for her reaction, Snip shot off into the grass, following a track that only he could sense. Second Son felt warmth within her for the first time since she knew her son had been taken. The dog, even so young, knew its master's scent, and he obviously was trailing Billy Wolf as fast as his short legs could travel.

This being so, Yellow Hair, her brother, and Lightning could take action to recover the horses if they knew the boy was safely out of the camp. She trusted her own ability to create a howl that only one of her own recognized as an imitation.

She paused, cupped her hands to her mouth, and quavered a long, mournful coyote wail into the night. In the distance beyond the creek a real animal answered her, and even farther beyond that another took up the cry.

From nearer—downstream, she realized—still a third "coyote" sang to the moon. Cleve or her nephew; they did it exactly alike, for the boy had taught her husband the art.

She turned after the pup, now almost out of sight and trackable only by the quiver of grass as he passed through it. The animal was moving quickly, but she caught up without effort and together they went forward after Billy Wolf.

The moon was going down now, and the night was getting darker, particularly amid the buffalo grass. Second Son stayed with the dog as much by sound as by sight, but the little animal never slowed. His tail no longer wagged, so intent was he upon following his nose, which was close to the ground. From time to time he paused, circled, sniffing hard, and took off in a new direction.

The track had veered to the west for a time, Second Son noted, and she knew her son had lost his bearings in the tall grass. But he had realized his error, for before long he turned north again, and she felt a surge of pride at his intelligence.

Behind her, distant now, there came a furious yell, followed by shrill cries and whinnies. She smiled without taking her gaze from the dim shape of the dog. Cleve and Singing Wolf and Lightning were at work getting back the horses of the Burning Hearts. It would be good to return with her son and the mounts as well.

The sky was alight with stars, but the ground was now invisible. She listened for the sniffing of the dog, the whip of his tail against stalks, the pad of his paws. Then, without warning, all those sounds stopped. There was an instant of intense silence and then the puppy gave a short and joyful yip.

Second Son hurried forward, stumbled over the furry body, and fell onto her knees beside a warm shape, which was fast asleep in a nest of grass. Her anxious hands felt him over from heels to scalp. The familiar salt-sweat smell of tired little boy filled her nostrils, and the fierce love she felt for her child almost overwhelmed her for an instant.

But she did not allow that to distract her. She shook him gently. "Billy Wolf! Wake, my son! Billy Wolf!"

He was usually easy to awaken; he must have been exhausted, for it took her some minutes to shake him awake. When he sat up at last, his hands flying out to protect himself from attack, she said, "It is your mother. And Snip. We have come for you. Now get up, for we must go back to find your father and your uncle and Lightning. We have all come after you, but they are busy getting back our horses."

"Fighting the Shinni?" were the first words out of his mouth. "Let's go right now. I want to shoot an arrow into that warrior who took me away. He made me wet myself because he wouldn't let me down to piss."

Second Son dissolved into laughter, as much from relief as from amusement. What a young warrior she had borne! He was indeed one of the Tsistsistas as well as his father's true son. If he grew to manhood, he would be one to reckon with.

When she had her laughter under control, she took him up, despite his wriggling and protests, and carried him swiftly back toward the stream, where her people must be engaged in wresting their animals from the raiders.

Soon the boy realized that she could go far more quickly than he could hope to and stopped his impatient movements. She put him on her back, his arms about her neck and his legs wrapped around her waist.

The smell of her son mingled with the scent of dried blood still staining the front of her sleeveless leather shirt. Beneath the stars she ran, the pup lolloping after her, panting with exertion and excitement.

Before she came to the creek, she could hear the *whick* of arrows in the still night. She dropped down into the ravine and moved downstream far enough to put her below the sound of conflict, and there she found a thick growth of young cottonwoods that allowed her to climb out into cover.

The boy followed her, quiet and intense. Together they crouched at the top of the bank, peering into the darkness.

If they were not to move out into the midst of their ene-mies, they must first find their own people.

Beyond a dark bulge that was either rocks or bushes there was a mixture of grunts, yells, and harsh breaths that told her a struggle was taking place there. Only when she caught a smothered curse did she know that Yellow Hair was one of the combatants, and she eeled across the rough ground beneath the fringe of cottonwoods, crawled to the top of the stony ridge, and peered down into the shallow cup beyond it.

A shape loomed against the sky as someone stood for a moment. Not one of her own, she could tell by the silhou-ette against the stars. Before she could ready an arrow, there came a thump, and the shape went down as if struck senseless.

"I threw a rock," said a small voice beside her. "That wasn't my father or the others. Did I kill him?"

She almost laughed again, but there was work to be done. Others still wrestled and groaned below them. "You did well," she said, and launched herself into the dim mass of motion beneath the rocks.

Almost at once she smelled her husband—his scent was as familiar to her as her son's—and yelled a fierce greeting as she caught the hair of the man who had him pinned down and cut his throat, almost in the same motion.

"Welcome," came the familiar voice as his big shape came upright and caught her up to throw her back onto the rock. "You go and help your brother. He has the horse herd moving toward home, and they're all upset and try-ing to break and run all over the place. I'm keeping these buzzards occupied until he gets well away."

She realized that no other shape but one was in the cup

of rock, a small one huddled against the rock so as to escape the notice of his father. "Billy Wolf!" she said, her tone sharp. "Come with me!"

The boy knew too well that one did not ignore Second Son when she spoke so, and he rose beside Cleve and tugged at his leg. "I want to stay and kill Shinni," he said.

Cleve caught him up and handed him to his mother. "You go with your uncle and keep the horses from running away. Lightning has been around on the other side, making them think there are a lot more of us than we really have.

"In a minute he's going to come sliding through here on his way to the creek, and we need to have our horses waiting on the other side. You help your mother get them there. All right?"

Not only was this an argument the boy would respect, it was an excellent plan in and of itself. Whatever Comanche were left would be furious and confused and ready to deal out death. Having the horses near at hand might possibly save the lives of her nephew and her husband.

"Come with me!" said Second Son.

She did not look back, but she could hear his bare feet pattering on the ground under the trees. She also heard Cleve's heavier tread moving the other way as he went to meet Rakes the Sky with Lightning.

If they survived, this would be a raid to talk about around the fires in winter lodges for generations to come. If they did not, they would die with honor, and no one could ask for more.

Cleve didn't really expect to rejoin his wife and son when they brought the horses. At least a dozen Comanche remained alive, though they were scattered about the site of the camp and out in the grass beyond the creek. He had heard nothing from Lightning for some time, and he had a cold feeling that the boy might have been killed or badly wounded after driving the horses into Singing Wolf's waiting hands.

But Second Son and Billy Wolf were safe. That was the great thing. His brother-in-law would teach the boy things that Cleve would never know, and Second Son would take her place again with her people, perhaps becoming the chief she had it in her to be. It was a shame his mother and brothers would never meet his boy, but if Cleve had learned one thing since leaving Missouri, it was that things never turned out as you expected.

He listened intently until the last whisper of sound, and there was very little to hear, had died away. Now his people were crossing the ravine. Now they were climbing the farther bank to the grassy plain beyond.

Soon they would be with Singing Wolf; if Second Son's kinsman judged it too dangerous for his "brother" and his son to return with horses for those behind them, he would keep them safe with him. Second Son was brave and loyal, but she was not foolish; she would listen to her brother.

The ridge of rocks ran at an angle from the creek into the grass, and Cleve flattened himself there and began crawling in the direction Lightning had taken. Angry yells from Comanche who were still looking for their attackers and their captive told him that a number were moving about the area, but he persisted until he found himself at the edge of the campsite.

He raised his head cautiously and peered over a slab of rock. The sky was so bright with stars that even with the moon down he could see faint patches of black on gray where warriors had abandoned their parfleche bags of supplies when he and Lightning came thundering past with the horses.

One man-shape was moving in that space, crouched but still visible as a curving back and a feathered headband against the stars. Cleve waited, for the man was approaching the rocks behind which he was hidden.

He silently tensed his legs for a spring, his knife ready in his fist. As the Comanche stepped up onto the stony out-crop Cleve rose like a grouse from his hiding place and knocked him flat on his back on the ground he had just left. Before the Comanche could grunt, the knife sliced across his throat, almost severing his head.

Cleve rose, crouching in his turn, and ran across the trampled space where the warriors had slept. The tall grass beyond was waving wildly, the tips black against the stars. Grunts of effort combined with the sounds of flesh slipping on flesh told him that two struggled there, and one must be his nephew.

He dashed into the grass and dived onto the struggling heap down by the roots. An arm came into his grasp, and Cleve grabbed it and pulled with all his might. The war-rior was much lighter than he and came up like a cork out of a bottle. It certainly wasn't Lightning—he was big-boned and well muscled, even as young as he was.

Without pausing, he swung the lighter man over his head and released him, letting him fly into the clearing, where he lit with a thump. As he tried to rise Cleve tackled him, and they rolled together in the dusty grass, the Co-manche trying to set his teeth in the white man's flesh or his fingers in his eyes.

But Cleve was heavier, much bigger, and he had years of life-and-death struggles behind him. Once he got the young warrior between his hands, the boy's neck snapped with an audible click.

As Cleve bent over the man still lying in the grass, Lightning's panting breaths turned into words. "Thank you, my uncle! I have taken an arrow through my side, and that little warrior was going to kill me."

"I thought we'd lost you," Cleve said, reaching to pull

the younger man to his feet. "And now we'd better get our tails out of here. The rest of these bastards are going to get their heads together, if we give 'em time, and take out after us like a pack of wolves."

Lightning touched his arm, bent double, and took off toward the line of cottonwoods. He moved quickly, but it was obvious that he was wounded, for he listed to one side.

Cleve followed him, glad to be out of that cleared spot in the grass. He didn't want to be there when the rest of the Comanche decided to get together and found their dead companion in the middle of things. Nothing made them more ferocious than the loss of warriors.

They fell into the ravine gratefully, grabbing at rocks as they slid downward. When Cleve's feet reached the shallow water of the creek, he grabbed Lightning and swung him around piggyback. Understanding at once, the youngster hooked his legs around his uncle's waist, and Cleve set out at a fast trot down the cut toward the spot at which they had entered it. Second Son would be waiting along their back trail with the horses.

From overhead came a hiss of breath, and Yellow Hair ducked behind a rocky angle. Lightning's bow flicked his ear as he rose to his knees and it came into position. Cleve waited for some signal as to what the boy wanted him to do.

A nudge of the left knee on his bent back told him to move in that direction, and he sidled from behind the rock, just enough to clear the aim of his rider. Lightning braced himself, the cross-drawn bow just clear of his steed's hair. He could hear the boy's quick breath of pain from his wounded side; the arrow's breeze touched Cleve's cheek as it left the bow.

Lightning settled back with a gasp. Beyond the knee of rock there came an echoing gasp, then a splash as someone fell into the water. Cleve listened hard, but only the bubble of water against some obstruction came to his ears.

He took time, then, to set Lightning on his feet, holding him with one arm while he checked the youth's wound with his free hand. Blood was already drying in sticky patches on the boy's skin.

The shaft of the arrow was a nuisance, however, though Lightning had already broken off much of its length. Cleve took the remaining stub between his fingers and snapped it off clean, almost even with the skin. The boy grunted almost without sound. His knees gave; Cleve caught him up, put him over his shoulder, and moved forward around the protecting angle.

The creek caught the glimmer of starlight from the sky, but its wavering ribbon was interrupted by a shape lying in the shallow flow. Ribbons of starlight outlined a man.

The smell hanging in the air was that of a Comanche. Cleve knew that without any doubt, for he had just gone hand-to-hand with a couple of them and their smell still clung to his skin.

He went cautiously but with speed. No other enemy appeared against the gleam of water, and if there was someone hiding beyond a bend, he had no time to worry about that. His knife was in his hand, his senses alert. If any warrior could outthink him or move faster than he, then he was welcome to take his blood.

A faint rim of light was beginning to show in the east, forerunner of dawn. They must be gone or else in hiding before the sun rose, for the remaining Comanche would scour the plain once daylight came. They had lost at least half their number, and their hearts would cry out for vengeance.

He found the animal track down which he and Lightning had come in the night. It was not easy to lift the boy high enough to lay him on a ledge near the top, but he managed it. Then he climbed out and reached down, blessing his long arms, to bring him up.

Lightning sighed, and his eyes opened. In one glance he saw the time and the place. Without a sound he gestured for Cleve to help him to his feet, and together they fled into the grass, following the flattened stems that were already rising again to their original position along their former trail.

A whicker came to Cleve's ears, and he paused, touching Lightning on the shoulder. He whistled softly, giving the morning call of a dove. A reply came from just ahead, and he dared to stand upright at last, tugging his wife's nephew along as he dashed for the sound.

He smelled the horses before he saw them. Their acrid scent was mixed with another that he knew. Second Son was there, waiting.

She had the mounts turned, ready to take off at once, by the time he reached her. Together they heaved Lightning onto his mount, now rested and ready to move, and he managed to sit as they leaped onto their own horses and headed northward after Singing Wolf and Billy Wolf and the horses.

A broad track showed where they had passed, and there was no point in trying to hide the trail of these three latecomers. Cleve dug his heels into Socks's sides, and the gelding flew after Shadow, while Lightning brought up the rear. Cleve kept glancing back to check on him, but the boy was riding steadily, without slumping.

Behind them came a cry filled with fury and threat: the Comanche had found another of their dead. As one, the three ducked below the grass tops and urged their mounts to further effort. They must find a defensible spot before the remnants of the raiders came after them.

The trail lay ahead, making straight for the Burning Heart village. Singing Wolf would, Cleve knew, make it there as quickly as possible and he would bring warriors back along his trail. They must fight off those who would want to take back what they had lost and to count coup on those daring to deprive them of their loot.

Ahead there was a knoll on which no grass seemed to grow. Thinking back, Cleve realized that he had noticed a complex of buffalo wallows on and around it as they came southward.

He called to Second Son: "If we go up there, we will be hidden in the wallows. We can shoot the Comanche with arrows, but they will have a hard time hitting us."

In reply, she veered Shadow toward the little hill, and Cleve slowed to let Lightning pass, checking the boy's condition as he went by. He was sitting straighter, though he held himself stiffly, fighting the pain of the embedded arrow in his side.

The first thing was to get that arrowhead out of the boy, Cleve realized, and there just might be time while they waited for the Comanche to come. He looked up at the sky. The sun was moving up, the slanting light making ever-shorter shadows across the prairie. The line of cottonwoods along the creek had sunk below the horizon.

He pulled Socks up beside Shadow, and Lightning's sorrel paused beside him. The top of the hill was sandy, the wallows deep from years of use. Buffalo chips lay scattered about them, and the strong smell of urine told Cleve that a bunch of the big animals had been here recently.

Lightning slid from his horse and stood beside the sorrel, clinging to its braided mane. Under his coppery skin there was a sick grayness that told of considerable blood loss. Second Son stepped beside him and eased him down into the nearest wallow, leaning him back against the shady side. Cleve took from Socks's back the waterskin Singing Wolf had sent with the returning mounts. He knelt beside the younger man and tilted a stream of liquid into his mouth.

Lightning swallowed, licked his lips, and opened his eyes. "You have the boy?" he asked.

"Billy Wolf is with my brother," said Second Son. "We will wait here, for the horses must rest. If the Comanche come, we will be well protected as they attack. But Singing Wolf will come back with people from the village. No one can guess which group will arrive first."

Second Son gazed southward over the tops of the waving grasses. Distant specks marked small groups of mule deer, and darker, more solid ones were grazing buffalo in small herds that had split off from the thundering masses that sometimes covered the plain with their shaggy bodies.

"When the beasts begin to move away, we will know the Shinni are coming," she said. "When the birds fly up from the grass we will know they are near. Until then we should rest."

Suddenly Cleve knew how exhausted he was. He had ridden and run and fought and slithered through grass all the night long. Now it was time to stretch out and gather fresh energy for whatever might come next.

chapter
— 6 —

The sun rode high, nearing noon. Second Son, lying on the edge of the grass beyond the southernmost wallow, was glad of the shade. Near the complex of dusty holes her man and her nephew also had sought the grass as protection from the sun.

From time to time she set her ear to the dusty soil beneath her, listening for the regular beats of horse hooves. So far, only the random stamps of distant groups of animals vibrated in the ground. The wind, sighing through the grasses, was no distraction, for her trained ear eliminated any irrelevant sound.

There had been much to do, she was certain, before the Comanche could collect enough horses to start in pursuit. Some few would be left to gather up their dead, and of those several might be hard to find in the buffalo grass. She had hidden at least one of her victims so well that she wasn't certain she could locate him herself, should she go back and look.

The sun moved overhead and began its downward slide. Soon her brother would reach the village. It would take hours for warriors of the Burning Hearts to retrace his route, though they would come along his track more swiftly than he had traveled, not having so many horses to keep moving together in the right direction.

The Shinni might well win the race, even after catching spooked mounts and getting together a band to set off after their escaped quarry. Even as she thought that, Second Son felt something in her bones. Again she laid her ear to the ground, and this time the regular rhythm of the riders to the south could be sensed, more than heard, as the skin of the plain vibrated to their passing.

She whistled, more from habit than need, the call of a ground bird. In an instant two others answered her, identical calls that she would defy anyone to identify as false. Nodding, she eeled backward toward the wallows, and by the time she reached the topmost, Yellow Hair and Lightning were there to meet her. As she dug herself into the soft dirt, stacking dried buffalo chips neatly to one side in case there was need of fire later on, she kept an eye toward the south.

The southern approach to their position was bare, trampled clean by the animals that scratched their woolly hides and soothed their weariness here. As this was the only knoll of any height for miles in any direction, it commanded a long view of the surrounding plain. She felt with much satisfaction that no Shinni, however brave or clever, could possibly slip past the watching eyes of the three Tsistsistas.

She surveyed the south, Cleve the northwest, Lightning the northeast. Anyone riding or even crawling through the grass, which was grazed rather short by the buffalo in most places near them, would be detected at once.

The thud of the approaching hooves grew more distinct as time passed and the sun slid deeper into the west. The shadow of her lance, when she stood it upright in the sandy soil, was a hand longer, then another half hand, before she could see the line of riders far to the south. She gave a grunt of warning, but neither of the men turned from his own area.

The Shinni were crafty and wise in warfare. Over the years they had gone horse stealing to the north and the Tsistsistas had raided southward, the tribes learning to respect the skills of each other as they stole horses and raided villages. In actuality, few deaths had resulted, for killing was not so much honor as counting coup or stealing a fat batch of mounts.

Second Son grimaced. Children were stolen constantly and reared as members of the raiding tribes. That was nothing that anyone became too incensed about, but this was *her* son who had been stolen. That was enough to justify killing, no matter how many deaths or how much blood it required to keep him safe and with his own people.

If the Shinni thought this just another raid and just another party recapturing stolen ponies, they must think again. Her brother and her son would be in the village by now, and the Burning Hearts needed no further warning to be on guard against attack. Billy Wolf was safe.

Those who now rode northward on his track were not. She intended to see them lying in the grass with the vultures picking at their eyeballs before she allowed them one step nearer to her people.

They came fast once they saw the horses, which, though picketed in the deepest cover possible to the north of the wallow, were easily detected in the short grass. But the leader, a tall, thin fellow on a piebald pony, was no fool and evidently knew the Tsistsistas from old conflicts.

The accuracy of the People's aim was equaled only by the heat of their blood in battle, so he pulled up his warriors, seven in all, well out of range and sent two of them scuttling away through the buffalo grass. Second Son knew they were circling wide under cover to come at the horses unnoticed, leaving the defenders of the wallows afoot.

That was just as well, for it delayed the attack for as long as it took the flankers to get into position. Meanwhile the Burning Hearts, following her brother, would be riding as fast as possible toward the place where they might meet their kindred.

The sun went lower, its shadow now stretching three hand lengths from the upright lance. Second Son took up her bow and checked the string, laid her clutch of arrows handily at her elbow, and made ready to do battle. Her lance was waiting, her knife ready. More than one of the Shinni would die when they came against her.

Sunk low in the wallow, Second Son watched the undulations in the grass that marked the passage of those sent to crawl around the knoll. The thin warrior sat his horse some bowshots distant, observing his prey and waiting for his men to get into place.

Behind her there came a whinny and the scuffle of hooves in the dust. She smiled, knowing that Cleve had brought their horses into the protective ring of wallows. No Comanche scuttling through the grass would have a chance to cut them loose and drive them away. If things got too hot, the three of them could mount and fight their way out of the ring of riders that would soon surround them.

There came a hiss from Lightning. The *whick* of an arrow told her he had seen one of the men sent to take their horses. She hoped his aim was true, and knowing her nephew, she felt it would be.

Now she was lying with her eyes even with the edge of the wallow, her shoulders tense. The one on the piebald lifted a hand, and she knew he had received some signal from those behind the knoll. The four men beside him heeled their ponies and strung out in a line; three circled to the right, two to the left, their orbits nicely spaced and well out of range of arrows.

They circled closer, and when the piebald came within reasonable bowshot, Second Son readied an arrow. Her first shaft went into the ground short of her target. She waited, hearing behind her the thrum of the others' bowstrings. A horse screamed, but it was fear and pain, not death, that was in its voice.

She loosed another shaft, this one at a smaller warrior on a pinto. He dropped onto the other side of the horse, hanging by one foot secured in the rope around the belly while he aimed his short bow under the animal's neck. His arrow went wide, which was a frequent problem when firing in motion from such a precarious position.

Her own fell short of the mark. She wasted no more arrows until a big gray came well within her range. The rider dropped beyond its other side and was thrown clear when the animal reared and bolted, her arrow deep in his haunch. She had another ready, and the Shinni went down with it through his neck.

A grunt told her that one of her fellows had taken a wound, but there was no time to attend to that now. The Comanche circled nearer and nearer, their arrows whizzing like hornets about the ears of those in the buffalo wallows. These were fine bowmen and riders, comparable even to the Tsistsistas. It was time to do something to change the situation.

Second Son backed away, flattened herself to slither across the ridge separating her wallow from the one behind the knoll, and dropped into the hollow with Cleve. "Is the fire gourd still on Shadow?" she asked.

"No. Here. I thought we might need it."

That was Yellow Hair, always thinking ahead. She took the stoppered gourd from him and crawled back to her former position. The dry chips were stacked ready to hand, and she ducked into the deepest part of the hole and kindled a small fire, crumbling bits of dried dung into the thin tendril of blaze.

Once she had it going, she held a large plate of the stuff in the flames until it blazed. Then she pitched it beyond the dusty complex of wallows, sailing it into the edge of the grass. A crackle began immediately, and she followed that first chip with more, working her way around the knoll. Every chip was burning fiercely, and soon smoke rose, white and acrid, obscuring the riders who circled beyond. That would hide the Tsistsistas from view as well.

She rose, unobserved she was sure. "Mount and ride!" she whispered to Cleve. She went forward and gave the word to Lightning, who leaped onto his sorrel at once.

The three, now coughing and choking from the smoke, kicked their mounts into motion and broke through the edge of the smoldering grass together. Two riders were passing at that moment. Lightning skewered one on his lance and Cleve knocked one off his horse with a massive fist.

Yips told them that the others were coming, but the way, for the moment, was clear; the rested horses thundered through the spreading ring of fire and smoke and headed north in single file. Second Son, riding last, turned to see who followed.

Only three warriors could be seen, bent low over the braided manes of their mounts and riding hard. One was the thin chief on the piebald, she made sure, before she turned again and let Shadow show her heels to the pursuers.

Ahead, Yellow Hair's braided crown was like flame in the sunlight, which now slanted long from the west. Lightning, just behind him, rode stiffly, and she knew he was the one who had been hit a second time, back there in the wallows. But he sat solidly and she could see little blood on his dark skin. His left arm was tucked close to his side, dark streaks running down and dripping from his elbow, and she suspected the arrow had gone through the meaty part of the upper arm.

The prairie rolled away beneath the hooves of the horses, and those behind began to fall back, their mounts, ridden hard and not rested, beginning to flag. She raised her voice in a derisive yell, *"Yi-i-i-i-i-i-i-i-i-eeeh!"*

Shadow picked up her dainty hooves and gained ground until she drew even with Lightning. He grinned at her as she passed, and Cleve turned his head to nod.

The mare, ready to run after her long rest, pulled away ahead of Socks, whose steady gait could last for hours but whose sprinting days were behind him. Shadow raised her head. Her ears flicked forward, and she whinnied a greeting to horses that her rider could not as yet see.

Again Second Son yelled, this time the long call of the Burning Hearts. It was answered from beyond the swells lying to the north. Her brother was there, and her people.

She gentled the mare to a walk and turned her at last to face their enemies. Cleve and Lightning, realizing what she was doing, did the same. Together they faced the Shinni, now equal in number and riding exhausted animals.

It was time to attack.

Before the approaching Comanche could determine what they were doing, the three kicked their mounts into a gallop and sped toward them, strung out side by side, their bows ready and their arrows in their teeth. Shaft after shaft zipped toward the oncoming riders, who veered off to left and right.

Second Son kneed Shadow toward the piebald, who was running free, his rider having slid off into the grass, which here was almost as tall as the head of a mounted warrior. Before she reached the area where the grass leaned against the wind as her quarry passed through it, she slid from her own mount and went into a crouch.

Now she had her knife in her hand, her bow again strung across her back. She crawled forward, pausing from time to time to listen for rustling in the grass. Her adversary, she knew, was doing the same. Her people had fought his over many years, and they knew what to expect.

She peered through a thick screen of stalks to catch a hint of motion beyond. Frozen into place, she waited, while the wind sighed above her as it swept over the grass tops. The movement came again, subtle, a mere shifting of the growth. But it was not caused by wind, and if it had been a rabbit, the creature would have moved differently.

She pulled her knees beneath her, tensed, and sprang. Crashing through the half-dried stalks, she fell full length atop the thin warrior who had led the Shinni. He squirmed like a snake beneath her, and her knife missed his neck and stuck deeply into the ground. She grappled with him, trying to pin him down while she freed the blade, but he was bigger than she and hard to hold.

She gave it up and let him pull her tightly against him. Once her nose was buried in his throat, she bared her teeth and went after his jugular, chewing through the man's taut skin and gnawing into the tough vein beneath.

Her victim gave a sharp gasp and began trying to free himself from this biting demon, who now hugged him as closely as he'd held her. Like a tick on a deer she clung, arms around his chest, legs locked around his, leaving no space to get a hand between them.

The gush of blood, when it came, almost drowned her, but she held her breath and kept biting, while the thin body struggled and rolled. When the Shinni moved no longer, Second Son rose and spat hot blood, wiping her lips on a handful of grass.

She was soaked with gore. The copperish scent rose around her, attracting hordes of flies, which had been busy with random carrion or buffalo dung dropped nearby on the prairie. This new feast brought them in zinging clouds, and Second Son crawled back into the grass, leaving the body to them.

She wrinkled her nose as she stood and ran toward Shadow. The whipping stems wiped away some of the blood from her skin; she hated the stench of it and always had. Even her mare shied as she approached, smelling death on her rider.

But Second Son put a stern hand on the horse's neck and sprang onto her back, turning her toward a bobbing blur amid the grass. That was Cleve's head, his yellow hair and new-grown beard gleaming in the sunset light. Even as she watched he dived off Socks onto someone afoot, and she urged Shadow toward him.

By the time she arrived he was standing, his whistle bringing Socks back to his side. She pulled up and looked down at the huddled shape that had been one of the Shinni.

Lightning, even with a wounded arm, would not be easily overcome, but she glanced about to spot him. His sorrel stood some yards distant; a desperate disturbance of grass not far from the horse showed where that conflict had taken place.

Cleve looked up, one eyebrow quirking in his familiar fashion, before turning to go to her nephew's aid. In a few moments both men returned, bloody and scratched. All three, she decided, were filthy and winded, but they were alive and the enemy raiders were dead, except for those who had been left behind by the stream to tend their other casualties.

Shadow flicked her ears and whinnied. Second Son

turned to look back to the north, where the first of the Burning Heart warriors had just appeared as specks topping the swells. Above them, buzzards were already wheeling in slow circles, waiting to descend upon the fallen.

She raised her arm and shrilled a cry of victory. Her brother's voice answered as the Tsistsistas pounded toward her, their lances ready, their bows strung for the battle that was already fought and won.

Again she cried out, her voice rolling across the prairie to greet them. Her son was safe, and all three who had pursued the raiders were returning to their village.

It was a good day to live as well as to die.

chapter

— 7 —

The prairie was still, except for the howl of a distant coyote and the chirr of insects. A high layer of thin clouds
blurred the stars, and the moon made a wash of paleness
through them. The Burning Heart village, moved instantly
from its previous location to one more remote, lay in a fold
of land beyond the river, and many watchers lay in the
grass on the highest of the swells, their senses alert.

Cleve and Second Son had not reconstructed their tipi
but lay on a thick buffalo hide retrieved from the collapsed
shelter. Billy Wolf, lying between them, twitched in his

sleep from time to time, reliving in his dreams, Cleve figured, the wild adventures of the day before.

The boy was able to rest, but the father was not. Still shaken by the narrow margin by which his son had been recovered from the Shinni, Cleve stared up into the milky sky, thinking of what might have happened if Buffalo Horn had not seen his grandson just before the raid began.

They might not have missed the boy in the confusion following the attack until it was too late to find him. It was possible that the pursuing party might have recovered the horses without ever knowing that Billy Wolf was abroad in the high grass. The thought made a cold sickness settle in Cleve's stomach. To lose his son . . . that would be as bad as losing his wife.

Unable to sleep, he crept from beneath their deerhide covering at last and moved away from the huddle of lodges. He was shaken, that was the problem. Knowing the perils of this wild country, understanding the long-lasting enmities between its peoples, until now he had not realized how those elements might endanger his child.

His mother had never seen her grandson. By now, of course, she might have others, for his brothers were old enough to be married and fathers. Yet he knew that she must grieve for him—how much he had never realized until he had a child of his own. She could not know if he still lived, for he had no confidence that the random messages he'd sent back east with traders and travelers might ever reach her.

Cleve had no desire to return to Missouri. His father would be there, he was certain, still harsh of eye and hard of hand. It was doubtful if he had forgiven his rebellious son or ever would.

And yet he found within himself a longing, strong and sharp as the cutting edge of a blizzard, to go back over the plains, following the river east to the Missouri country where he had spent most of his childhood. He wanted to show his son the places that had comforted him when he fled his father's wrath into the woody fastness. He wanted to show his mother this strong child who was bone of her bone.

And he was afraid. Ma was a woman of her people and had always feared and detested Indians of any kind. She looked askance at any newcomer who was not the pale-skinned, freckled Scotch-Irish breed from which she sprang, and often skin shades were compared aloud as she sat mending socks and pants knees in the evening.

"That Miz Frazier, she looks mighty dark for an Irishwoman. Black hair, black eyes—touch of the tar brush there someplace, I'd swear. You take care you don't play with her young ones, Cleve. They're not our kind."

He could hear her voice, soft and musical, saying those cruel words. He had thought until he found himself among them that any Indian was a tool of Satan, a monster without feelings or kindness, without family or friend. Now that he knew better, he called into question all the strange little rules his mother had used for shaping her behavior toward others.

He'd learned the hard way that the shade of a man's hide was no indication of the color of his heart. Friends were found in unlikely places, wrapped in bodies that didn't conform to Ma's specifications. For every fur thief like Jules Terrebonne there was a good man like Emile Prevot to balance out the scale.

The devil, he knew from experience, came in Scotch-

Irish hues as well as darker ones. But still he wanted to go home. He wanted his brothers to know Billy Wolf. He wanted them to know Second Son. Until that happened, he knew there would be a big gap in his life, and he would never feel quite comfortable.

He and Second Son had talked about that at length while traveling down from the high country. His wife, wise beyond her years of experience, had noted many things about the white men among whom she spent every Rendezvous.

"Your people fear and hate mine," she told him. "They pretend to greet us, to trade with us gladly, but I can feel all about them a sharpness like the quills of a porcupine. They look at me and they see just a red-skinned woman pretending to be a man, one who needs to be brought down to the level of their bought women in the tipis. I feel their anger and their lust surrounding them in a fog that burns and freezes me."

He had never heard her admit to fear before, and thinking back on his own observations in the camps they'd shared, he understood with sudden certainty what she meant. After their first Rendezvous, when she had been attacked by many men and saved from rape only by Old Joe Ferris, the preacher who trapped in the mountains, she had gone cautiously, always armed, always alert.

"I believe that this is something inside your people. There are a few like Ferris who make friends and mean it, but most are hidden enemies, just waiting for a reason to quarrel and to attack us."

Those had been her words, and examining his knowledge of his own kind, he knew them to be true. Knowing his mother as he did, he was convinced that a Cheyenne wife would not be welcome or even tolerated in her home.

It made him sad and ashamed, for though the Tsistsistas warred with other tribes like the Pawnee and the Comanche, they adopted captives of many tribes into their own, if there was room for them. Those they tortured were enemies who would have done the same to them with equal enthusiasm, and there seemed, as far as he could tell, to be nothing personal in the ritual.

Indeed, Second Son had told him tales of particularly heroic sufferers who had aroused the admiration of the entire band by the way they endured torture before they died. Their names went into the long tales, and their courage was held up to children as examples of virtue to be copied.

The whites were objects of curiosity more than anything, he thought, to the people of the plains. Only when some of that kind behaved with typical brutishness and lack of honor had hostilities begun to be common between some tribes and the trappers and traders. He could imagine that by the time settlers began to move out into the grasslands, which was something almost certain to happen, there might be full-scale wars.

No, his mother was not fitted by background or personal preference to accept an Indian daughter-in-law. His father—he shivered at the thought—would be as likely to shoot her as not. After, of course, shooting his oldest son.

The boy should be safe, however. Neither of his parents would kill a child, though his father had done his share of beating his own young'uns. Surely, as he got older, Jase Bennett would have mellowed just a bit, Cleve thought.

His brothers were now old enough to step in, if needed,

so he wouldn't have to tackle Pa with a pitchfork again, as he had been forced to do in defense of his mother. As well as being what sent him up the river with the trappers, it might still pose a problem if he went home again.

A touch on his arm brought him back to the present, and Cleve turned with instant reaction to find himself looking down at Second Son. She had come silently after him, the whipping of the prairie wind covering the sound of her breathing. Now she stood beside him, her hand on his wrist, her head cocked to survey his face in the light.

"You are troubled," she said.

"I am. I'm thinkin' about what might have happened yesterday. We could have lost the boy, you know. I can't seem to get that out of my craw."

She sighed and stared toward the dark line of the horizon. "What happens happens, Yellow Hair," she said. "I have seen how white men worry about the past and what is to come, but I do not understand it.

"Nothing can be done to change yesterday. We acted, and all was well. But if it had gone badly, still there was nothing we could do to change that, either. It takes enough effort to stay alive. Wasting strength on such thoughts seems foolish."

Cleve knew that all too well. "And I can't do a damn thing about what's going to happen tomorrow, either," he said. "But I've got to take the boy back home and let him know his folks there. They're getting old, my ma and pa. Could be they're already gone, but I need to know for sure. I can give my son a chance to know his uncles, if nothing else. I've learned from you how important uncles and aunts can be. Can you understand that?"

Her hand was warm on his arm as she squeezed gently.

"Why do you think I wanted to come east this summer, after Rendezvous? I wanted him to know these of his kindred, too. I do understand, Yellow Hair. And I know that it would not be wise for me to go with you."

"I hate to leave you here. We haven't been separated for more than a few weeks since we got together back on the Belle Fourche. My God—seven years ago? Seems like yesterday." He could see no difference in her. She was, if anything, more beautiful than ever, he thought.

"Our son has seen six winters," she agreed. "Those have been good years, and I will miss you both, but there is work for me here in my brother's band. I will not be idle while you are gone." She leaned against him, and he put his arm around her square shoulders, feeling the wiry strength of her, breathing the aroma of dry grass and fresh oil and woman that was uniquely hers.

He would go east as soon as they could get the village back in order and when it was certain that no larger band of Shinni was going to come north to avenge the horse stealers.

How the journey would go was always a question in this untamed country. Its end might be as wild as anything about it, he thought, turning with his wife to their interrupted rest.

It took days to order the village again; reconstructing tipis meant long trips to the hills where lodgepole pines grew. Those who had been wounded were tended, and some mended while others slid away into death. The healers were busy, and Singing Wolf seemed to be everywhere, seeing that all was done well for his people.

Second Son slipped almost unnoticeably into the position of her brother's right hand, Cleve saw with some amusement. Buffalo Horn did not recover his strength after the raid, his age seeming suddenly even greater. The elders who survived were wounded or ill, so the burden would have fallen totally upon the peace chief if Second Son had not been there.

Cleve loaded packs with gifts for his people. Buffalo robes, fine beaver plews saved from the last winter's trapping, a lynx fur that would keep his mother warm in winter went into the bundle, along with the bag of gold he had retrieved for them. Odd figures carved by the old men of the Burning Hearts were included, for there might be young nephews or nieces who would like such gewgaws.

When, one morning, Cleve decided that the time had come to begin the eastward journey, Billy Wolf was bouncing with excitement. His peers in the band were envious of this long trail that he was about to take, and he promised faithfully to remember everything and to tell them every foot of the way when he returned.

Cleve and Second Son sat together in their newly repaired tipi, saying little but thinking much. When they rose, their hands touched for a moment, warm and solid, and then they parted.

The two Bennetts rode away without looking back, though Cleve felt his wife's gaze on his back until they crossed the next swell and the village dropped out of sight.

He raised his head, drinking in the clean wind that swept endlessly over the buffalo grass. It had been very long since he turned his face toward the Missouri, and as they followed the Cheyenne River toward its confluence with the greater stream, he felt a tickle of excitement beneath his own rib cage.

What were his brothers like now? Was his mother still alive and well? And his father ... was Jase Bennett the cruel and heavy-handed patriarch he remembered, or had he, too, felt the touch of time and mellowed with age?

In a few weeks they would know. Before snow flew, they should reach the Little Sac River and the farm that had been his home when he was the age of his son.

Cleve kicked Socks into a faster walk, and Billy Wolf, riding Blaze, the son of Second Son's old mare Shadow, grinned widely and did the same. Together they moved through the sea of grass toward Missouri.

It felt strange, riding across the grasslands with only his father, the horses, and his yellow pup, Billy Wolf thought. There had been some question about taking the little dog along, but Snip had become very necessary to the boy. Besides, his legs were getting longer by the day, and it was almost certain he could keep up.

"He can ride with me if he gets tired," he had pleaded.

For some reason that made Second Son look up at his father with an odd expression. A smile almost curved the corner of her lip, and she agreed that Snip might go. "It may be that he will be as useful as old Snip was to us," she said, laying a hand on the dog's quivering back.

Thinking of Second Son, the boy felt suddenly bereft. Never had he gone anyplace without the solid presence of his mother. They had always traveled with him securely in the middle, either his father or mother riding ahead and scouting out the country and the other riding behind, making sure that no danger threatened from the rear.

Now he and Cleve rode abreast, with the pack horse trailing behind on his line. Ahead was nothing but grass, long waves of it, swells of it, small hillocks and shallow hollows of it. It seemed to have no end and to run away into the edge of the sky itself.

Used to the mountains as Billy Wolf was, this seemed almost frightening. Again he had the feeling that he might fall upward into the sky, but he suppressed it and rode with a properly grim expression, as befitted one of the Tsistsistas.

Snip's tail bounced in and out of sight as the pup bounded through the grass, sometimes racing after a jackrabbit, sometimes waiting for the riders to catch up, at which point he would look up pleadingly for a ride. Billy Wolf thought he simply liked to look out over the tops of the growth through which he had to plow when on the ground. But the boy seldom refused to give the pup a rest on Blaze's back, where the little dog braced himself fore and aft with paws dug into the blanket that served as a saddle.

When days passed with only occasional creeks, dry now with midsummer, interrupting the endless stretches, the boy began to believe that they would never find their way out of the plains. Their waterskins grew limp, and they rationed their horses, as well as themselves, when it came time to drink.

Cleve reassured him as well as he could. "There are mountains in Missouri. Not great big busters like we've got back in the Absarokas, but real ones just the same," he promised. "And we have more water than you'd believe, creeks and rivers and lots of rain."

Only when they came over a swell and saw before them a long line of dark trees did the boy really believe they were actually making progress. The stream his father called the Des Cygnes was ahead, the trees along its course becoming larger as they approached. Soon even Billy Wolf could smell water, and the horses had long since picked up their ears and begun to hurry toward that grateful scent.

Snip raced ahead, yipping frantically after some creature in the grass that was faster than he. When they rode into the shade of the first trees, he returned to follow them down the near bank to the shelf of sand forming a small beach. Bushes and reeds grew along its edges, making a cool green spot for resting.

"Where are we?" the boy asked as they dismounted and led the horses to drink. "Are we to Missouri yet?"

Cleve smiled. "Almost. When we get across this river, we'll soon be on home ground. The Little Sac is just a few days farther now." He pulled Socks and Blaze and the packhorse out of the shallows and tied them to trees so they wouldn't drink too much all at once.

"Come here, son." He crouched over a patch of damp sand and scratched with a twig. "There's the mountains we came from, away back to the west and north." He put a round mark there. "About here's where the village was when we left it." A wavy line marked the river and an X the camp.

"We came all this way overland and cut off a many a mile." Cleve dotted a long line down at an angle until it drew a big square. Then he marked in a deep line running almost east and west. "And there's the big river I followed with Ashworth. This river is down about there, and here we are, right beside it. Over there a piece is Missouri."

"Do we cross right now?" Billy Wolf felt a sudden urgency to do just that.

"Too deep here. Rain from those clouds we saw in the east must have filled all the streams, and the water's too high. See how the river runs, no ripples, no eddies, just smooth rolls that romp along like a great big snake? That means she's deep and swift.

"No. We'll wait till we find someplace where you can see riffles and maybe a sandbar out in the middle. Someplace where it's shallow enough to cross so the horses won't get washed downstream. I've seen many a horse lost in many a river, back when I came away with Ashworth's trappers.

"Now we'll mosey along downstream and find someplace to camp that won't be likely for somebody to stumble over us. This country's getting to be plumb overcrowded with trappers and traders and hunters and warriors looking for game or plunder."

They remounted and turned to parallel the stream, keeping a fair distance from the water but staying in the shelter of the outlying trees. Horsemen showed up too plainly out on the grasslands, for their heads and shoulders bobbed up and down, dark against the tan grass, to catch the eye of any alert watcher.

The afternoon dwindled to evening, and the last sun lit towering clouds that seemed to move deliberately across the sky to the south. Cleve paused to watch. "My ma used to talk about ships with sails, moving slow and quiet across the ocean. I never saw them, and I doubt she did, but I have a feeling those look a lot like 'em. Did you ever see anything that took your breath more than that?"

Billy Wolf gazed at the sky, feeling a chilly lump in his middle. Even the mountains he knew so well were not so tall and white and awe-inspiring. He felt as if those shining clouds might be living creatures, going on a journey of their own for some purpose he couldn't even guess.

The sunset turned them to pinky gold, and then shadow crept up from below until the bases were purple black. Only the tops were bright, and the land below was covered with darkness.

Cleve turned aside up a runnel that drained into the river. A clump of cottonwoods and brush offered shelter from the wind, and in the bottom of the little ravine, where there was grass on either side of the shallow stream but in which their mounts would be hidden from anyone riding the plain at night, they tethered the horses on long leads.

"If it rains again upcountry, this thing could flood like the river itself," his father told the boy. "Got to fix it so the beasts can get up the bank and out of the way of any water that comes down.

"We'll camp up here on the shelf, out of sight. But we'll build no fire. The Osage and the Kansa, the Comanche and the Arikara and ninety-two other tribes travel up and down the rivers, and we don't want to run into any of 'em."

As he settled into his bedroll for the night the boy snug-

gled his back against his father and his front against Snip.
Long howls of coyotes and cries of strange birds filled the
darkness in this alien place, making him glad of company.

As he drifted into sleep he thought of tomorrow. Perhaps they would cross the river and find themselves in the
forest country where his father had been a boy. With that
in mind he slept, and even the rain didn't wake him as his
father pulled a heavy robe over them to keep off the wet.

He woke damp and achy, with Snip trying to scratch a
flea without getting out from under the shelter of the hide
covering. Billy Wolf scratched too, for his pup was not
stingy with his fleas. When they came to the river again,
he would wash, for he wasn't used to itching so intensely.

He rolled out and stood, stretching and yawning, while
his father shared out strips of jerky and drafts of water
from the smaller of the waterskins they carried. Munching
on the tough meat, Billy Wolf climbed onto Blaze and dug
his heels into the horse's sides. In the light of a damp
dawn, they started eastward again, and this time Cleve
seemed to know just where he intended to intersect the
river and cross.

They came out of the grassland following a dry wash,
which disappeared beneath big trees that were not cottonwood or aspen or fir or anything the boy had ever seen.
They had big dusty-green leaves shaped something like his
hand, and their trunks were very thick, the branches overhead curving downward as if with the weight of years.

Beyond the trees was the gleam of water under cloudy
skies, and the boy understood why his father had aimed
for this particular spot. In the middle of the stream was a
broad sandy patch, and above that was a disturbed stretch
from which the tops of rocks thrust above the water.

"I helped drive a herd of horses over this way for a neighbor back when I was a boy," Cleve muttered as they rode along the bank, searching for just the right place to cross. "If it hadn't been for this spot, we'd never have got across. When I was a bit older, I was with a bunch of men who hunted out this country for meat in a bad year, and I haven't forgot an inch of it."

He kneed Socks into the current along the bank, and there the river was deep. The gelding raised his head, his nostrils flared, and he swam strongly toward the white water and sand some yards away.

"You let me get set in the sandbar," Cleve said without turning his head. "I'll get Socks braced, and then I'll pitch you a line. You tie it onto your waist, real tight. The horses can swim out if they lose their footing, but this water'll turn you tail over teakettle and drown you if we give it a chance."

Billy Wolf didn't like the idea of being tied like a baby, but he had learned before he remembered anything not to question his parents' commands. Life often depended on instant obedience, and he had seen people die because they stopped to argue. Among the trappers that sort of thing was often talked about, and at almost every Rendezvous there was another tale of some greenhorn who had talked when he should have jumped.

The supple coil of line came sailing toward him, and he snagged it out of the air and secured the end around him. Then he, too, urged his mount into the water. Behind them the packhorse snorted with distaste, but the tug on his line brought him along behind Blaze.

When they reached the strongest current, a few lengths from the bank but still a long way from Socks's anchoring body, the boy felt his horse begin to work. The powerful shoulders heaved, and Blaze shook his ears and tried to keep his nose above the surging waves coming down between the rapids and the shore.

Billy Wolf felt a tug at the lead rope, which lay beneath his knee. At the same moment Cleve shouted, "Loose the packhorse!"

Instantly the boy cut the lead, keeping his lower legs tucked tightly into the leather rope fastened about Blaze's body. A panicked scream sounded from the horse behind, but he kept his gaze fixed on his father, and Cleve reeled him in, horse and all, as if he had been a fish.

"The horse . . ." Billy Wolf sputtered.

"He'll come ashore downstream. There'll be another sandbar further along, and he'll catch himself there and be mighty anxious to get back with familiar company. Come on now. This patch isn't as rough as it looks, and we'll be across before the sun's well up."

Subdued by his wetting and the loss of the other horse, Billy Wolf fell in behind Socks, watching where the older horse set his hooves and guiding Blaze in his tracks. Though water splashed high about their legs and seemed to try to wash them downstream, here it was too shallow, and the mounts came to the other shore, this one a mix of sand and pale stone, without mishap.

"We'll stop and let the horses rest here," Cleve said. "You want to go with me to round up old Patches, or you want to stay and watch the other horses?"

Billy Wolf thought for a moment. Then he said, "I'll keep watch. You want me to hide?"

Cleve beamed. This was, the boy knew, the sort of thinking his father approved. "Hide good, and don't come out until you hear my whistle. Better be a fish eagle, here. Some of the mountain birds don't come this far east. Sounds like this." He pursed his lips, and a shrill screech sounded among the trees, which seemed to grow more and more thickly on this side of the river.

Billy Wolf nodded. He'd know that sound whenever he heard it for the rest of his life. His people in the plains survived because they trained their ears to recognize such calls and to know if they were real or human.

"Two and one and two?" he asked. That was the usual pattern of calls that told those in his family that a signal came from one of their own.

When his father moved quietly away along the riverbank, he felt suddenly very much alone. Checking the trees, he chose a huge oak. Setting a toe in a crack in the rough trunk, he clambered upward until he reached the sprawl of branches two man-heights above the ground.

There he settled to watch the horses, which had now shaken their hides dry and were prospecting for grass and tender leaves among the ground cover under the trees. The quiet sounds of their movements mingled with the morning songs of birds and the chatter of water from the river. The boy found his eyelids growing heavy.

He woke with a jerk, for some sound struck an alien note and his trained ear caught it at once. A footfall crunched a leaf, a twig broke with a snap, and a grunting breath whuffed among the trees. As Billy Wolf stared down, a young black bear ambled out into the small glade and stared interestedly at the grazing horses.

Socks turned his head, his ears pricked forward. Blaze followed suit, but the bear was moving faster and faster toward them. Billy Wolf shrilled the whistle with which his father called Socks, and the horse turned from the attacking bear toward the tree as Blaze broke into the bushes and disappeared downstream.

The boy dropped out of his perch onto his father's horse and kicked him in the sides with desperate urgency. Socks sprang forward, leaped a fallen tree, and pounded after Blaze.

Behind them there came a roar of frustration. Billy Wolf could hear the bear coming, even above the thud of his heart and the crashing of his mount's hooves into the debris beneath the trees. He kicked harder, and Socks responded.

The boy gulped in air, pursed his lips, and tried to whistle. Too dry. Too breathless. Again he tried, and this time a rather faint replica of the call of the fish eagle came out. Two and one and two.

With more assurance, he repeated the signal, hoping his father would hear and come. A bear could run faster than you might think, and if Socks stumbled among the deadfall through which he was running, they would both be in trouble.

In the distance he heard a whistle. It was repeated, and he knew Cleve was coming. Socks whinnied suddenly, and Billy Wolf knew his father must be riding the packhorse. The gelding had recognized the other animal, even through his terror.

A rider passed them, heading toward their pursuer, and the boy began gentling Socks to a walk, then to a halt. They were both breathing deeply as he turned back on his tracks.

There was another roar, this one of pain, and Billy Wolf came through the thick growth in time to see an arrow sink into the neck of the bear. Another *whicked* from the bow, and the light of fury died out of the creature's eyes. It sank into a huddle of dark fur, and the boy dropped from the horse and ran to look down at it.

Cleve put his hand on his son's head. "Lots of meat there," he said. "It's only about two more days to the Little Sac. Might be we can skin out this critter and take a mess of bear with us when we go. Pa always was pleased when visitors brought their own food. You game?"

Billy Wolf looked up, eyes wide, and nodded emphatically. Although some of the Indians he had met at the Rendezvous considered the bear a brother, not to be killed or eaten, his own kind relished the meat.

"We'll take our own grub," he said, imitating the tone he had learned from Old Joe Ferris.

Cleve laughed and turned to call for Blaze, who, though learning fast, was not yet entirely trained to his signals. Then the two of them set to work, and before dark they were bloody to the elbows.

But a fine black bearhide was stretched on the sand, pegged down for scraping, and strips of meat were drying beside a fire built deep in a hollow among the trees. They would bring not only gifts but meat. The boy felt that would surely earn them a welcome from these unknown kinsmen.

The long dry spell had been broken by a series of rains that swept down out of the plains and flung their fury at the woods and hills of western Missouri as if intending to wash them away. The Little Sac had been running bank full, and the boys had to drive the cattle out of the river-bottom pastures into the hills for fear of losing them when the big waters came down.

That left Mattie alone in the house with Jase, something that always depressed her. She wondered frequently, now that she was getting old, why she had married him. He wasn't all that well favored, for all his bright hair and good size, and he certainly hadn't been rich when he came through Kentucky on his way west to the fertile farmlands beyond the Mississippi.

She'd had the education to make her own way, which few women could claim. As a teacher she might have . . . but then she thought of her sons. Nothing she had suffered through these long years was bad enough for her to regret having her boys.

She gazed off the front porch. The bare-scraped yard was pale sand, shadowed blue by the overhanging oaks and elms and hickories. Her roses blazed with midsummer blossom, and the crepe myrtles were a froth of bloom. The irrepressible part of her that gloried in beauty warmed to a surge of feeling, but she quashed it and turned to the man sitting in the rattan rocker.

Jase Bennett had always been big, a strong, square man with arms of iron and a will to match. His temper had been legendary, and he had ruled her and his sons with his fists and his whip. Now he sat, pale and thin, his hands lying limp in his lap. His face was white, lined from cheekbone to jaw with the tracks of pain and frustration.

Those pale eyes that had been so apt to blaze with furious fires were blank as pewter plates, seeming unaware of the summer light struggling through the clouds to touch the colors of blossoming plants in the yard. The jaw that had jutted with determination now sagged.

When she spoke to him, she had to touch his shoulder to get his attention. Then his head swung toward her, his effort showing in the motion, and those blank eyes fixed their gaze on her and slowly recognized her presence. When she spoke, Jase's mouth hung slightly open, his lips moving as if repeating her words.

She seldom tried to communicate with him now. The relief of being free from his beatings and random cruelties had long become a habit for all of them, letting them forget what they had suffered under his domination. Now she felt only pity for the man, and guilt, for it had been her hand that struck him first with the ax handle, all those years ago. That had done some damage inside his head that had never been entirely healed.

Cleve . . . She sighed, thinking of her oldest, gone for so many years without any word returning across the plains to tell her if he lived or died. Jase would have killed the boy if he'd been let. She salved her conscience with that thought.

Once Cleve lifted his hand against his father, the only way he could survive was either to kill the man or to run. She had kept her son from patricide. That was the only comfort she had.

She turned into the house to stir the pot of beans on the iron cookstove that Eugene had brought her from St. Louis. After years of cooking over the fireplace, that was a great luxury, though she seldom used it, as if she might wear it out or break it by using it too often. A peep into the oven told her the cornbread and ham would soon be ready.

Tim would be hungry after his work with the cattle. Maybe Gene would stop by for supper before going on down the road to the house he shared with Sarah and their two daughters. At the thought of her grandchildren Mattie's heart warmed. Two little angels, towheaded and blue-eyed as children should be.

There came a hail from some distance, and she went again to the porch and peered between the overhanging fronds of trumpet vine and wisteria that draped the fence. The piebald mare was coming. Tim, her youngest and the comfort of her old age, was in time for supper.

Jase had turned in his chair at the sound of hoofbeats in the damp sand. For some reason, since his injury he had seemed to warm to his youngest, although it had been Tim's birth and the senseless accusations about his paternity made by Jase's mother that had turned the man sour and cold. The boy was the image of his father, and not even that wicked old woman could have called him a bastard if she could see him now.

The memory brought a flush to Mattie's face, as it always did. As if she'd had the time to dally, even if she'd had the inclination!

But that was dust now, dead with much else. Now her son was coming, and she must get supper onto the table. He would sniff the air and beam at her as if no food on earth was as tasty as hers. He knew how to please her, and he tried. That was something that Mattie constantly found astonishing.

There was entirely too much for the three of them, she knew, but food was not a problem here on this rich land. Game and hogs and cattle, gardens bursting with vegetables, fields with corn and potatoes and yams—no one willing to work need go hungry here, she thought. The pigs would relish what was left.

She heard Jase struggling to rise, and she hurried out to keep him from falling, as he often did. He didn't look at her, however, but stared down the road. The sun had gone behind the trees now, and the shadowed way was dim, but there seemed to be more than one rider approaching. Had Gene come for supper?

She held on to Jase's elbow, steadying him on his feet, but her attention was focused on the shapes of horses and riders now nearing the gate, half-hidden behind the screen of shrubbery and vines along the fence. One was a child. That was clear. One horse was loaded with a pack, so these were travelers.

Who had Tim brought along with him for supper? He had never done such a thing before.

She felt a queer reluctance to settle Jase back in his chair while she went to greet the newcomers. Since her cousin John had visited them long years ago, there had been only a handful of people who came to claim their hospitality. She felt strange now with people she didn't know.

The gate opened and Tim stepped onto the sandy path. He was beaming, his eyes alight, his teeth shining beneath his blond mustache. Behind him came a bigger man, young and blond—Jase! Her heart almost stopped.

And then she knew. It was her son Cleve, long lost and given up for dead. Heavier, solid of bone and muscle, long of hair, still it was her own son. Her blood knew it and her bones cried out their recognition before her mind really grasped the fact.

He was dressed in deerhide like an Indian, and his hair was long, braided, caught about her brow with a beaded band. She shivered, feeling an unnamed apprehension, but she ran down the steps to him; he caught her up, her feet dangling, in a great hug.

"Ma!" he murmured into her ear. "Ma, it's been so long!"

He put her down carefully, as if afraid she might break. She stepped back to stare up at him, but her hand clasped his as if fearing he might evaporate again into the wild country that had hidden him for so long.

Now the differences about him struck her. His eyes looked strange, as if he were used to seeing over great distances. He carried himself like a king, not like the cowed boy who had pitchforked his father and then run for his life.

There was no seemly humility to him at all, and her life-long conditioning had taught her that people must be humble before God. Somehow she didn't think he would kneel, even to pray, any longer. He hadn't the look of it.

Her heart hammering with dread and joy, she tugged him toward the porch. "Come say hello to your pa. You won't know him, son. He's . . . different now. We hit him too hard, I think, keeping him out till you could leave. He's never been the same since."

He resisted her pull and smiled down at her. "You've got somebody to meet too, Ma," he said. "I've got a son now. William Wolf Bennett. Brought him to see you specially. Come on, son. This is your grandmother."

The dread grew as she looked down at the small shape that came from behind his father. This was no Bennett—this was an Indian. The hair was pale brown with golden highlights, but the eyes were black. The skin was coppery brown.

The loincloth and moccasins, the deerhide shirt, the knife in a small sheath at his waist told her this was a savage, not any grandson of hers. But Cleve was smiling, watching, and she could not show her instant revulsion.

"Hello, William," she said, loosing her son's hand and extending her own toward the boy.

Those eyes were sharp, intelligent, knowing. The child

took her fingers in his as if a handshake was something alien to him. But he said, in passable English, "I am glad to meet the mother of my father. I am called Billy Wolf, after my father's friend Holy William and my uncle Singing Wolf."

The tone was so adult, the wording so formal that it took her off guard. This was no primitive animal, without manners or learning. Her long experience of teaching, first the local children before her marriage, then her own sons and her granddaughters, gave her an instinct for gauging the young.

What had her son brought home to her? She felt all her comfortable assumptions, learned over a lifetime, crumbling, but she tried to conceal her unease. "Come along and meet your grandpa," she said.

This time the group moved up the path to the porch, where Jase was leaning forward in his rocker, his mouth moving without making a sound as he stared at his oldest son.

Cleve paused, standing on the ground and looking up into Jase's eyes. Mattie had seen in his stance his dread of meeting again with his father; now his face was filled with shock at the old man's appearance. It was, she knew too well, like meeting the ghost of the man Jase had been.

"Pa?" His voice was unsteady. He cleared his throat and said again, "Pa?"

Jase leaned forward, his lips trying desperately to shape a word, to articulate a name, but he hadn't spoken a clear word since that day almost nine years ago when he had been struck down.

Yet his hands, so slow, so thin and weak, moved forward toward his son, and Cleve stepped onto the porch and caught the old man in a hug. "Pa!" She almost thought he was crying, but when he eased Jase into the chair again, there were no tears.

Cleve beckoned to the boy, who loosed her hand instantly and ran up the steps. "This is your grandfather," her son said. "Shake his hand, son."

To Mattie's amazement, Jase pulled the boy close and touched his face with a tentative finger. The man looked up at his son, and Cleve nodded.

"His mother is a Cheyenne, a warrior and a woman in a million. We were married by a Methodist preacher, and we have the papers." He glanced aside toward Mattie, and she knew he felt that she would be comforted to know his union with that savage woman had been lawful.

But that was not what troubled her. Mingling her blood with that of another race, a dark-skinned race, that was anathema. All her long ancestry rose up in her to protest this miscegenation, but she kept her lips shut tightly and said no word to show her revulsion and contempt.

Her son, taking up with a red whore! Warrior woman, indeed! Everyone knew women weren't soldiers.

She pushed past Tim, who was grinning indiscriminately at everyone present, and went into the kitchen, calling back, "I've got to get the beans off the stove. Bring your pa in and we'll eat."

She got out the remnants of the china she had brought from Kentucky, though she knew the boys and that wild child wouldn't appreciate it. She poured buttermilk from the crockery pitcher and buttered cornbread with a lavish hand.

She sliced ham and spooned out beans and greens from

their respective pots, and all the while her heart said, "No! No! No!"

But she smiled and sat at the table and noted with surprise that the child ate neatly, though he knew nothing about spoons. The plate met with his approval, and he filled it with food and dug in with his knife, making no mess and touching, when he had finished at last, the roses on her china sugar bowl with a gentle finger.

"That is pretty," he said.

With a jolt, she realized that no matter how alien this youngster might seem, her blood did, indeed, run in his veins. He had an appreciation for beauty, too. Would that forge some bond between them?

But again her heart said, "No! No! No!"

chapter
— 10 —

Although he had been accustomed to the steep green forests of the Rockies, Billy Wolf found the woods of this Missouri country very different. The rains that had given them so much trouble as they crossed the rivers had not diminished, and the ground was springy and moist, bursting with plants for which the boy had no names. The very greens of the trees had more of brown and gold in them than did the firs and aspens he knew.

They had traveled fast, as if his father felt an urge to reach his home country. The boy could understand his feelings, for already he was homesick for the steep gray heights of the Absarokas, their sudden glens thick with fragrant trees. Luckily they had met few people on the trails Cleve followed, and those were chance travelers like themselves, instead of tribes bent on raiding.

When they had crossed the Little Sac, Cleve stopped on the south side of the river, gazing about him as if puzzled at being so near his home again. "It's just the same," he had said, as if to himself. "Except for the river being so high, it's just like it was when I left. There's a tree down over there—looks like a tornado took it over. And the bushes and saplings have grown a lot. Still, it looks like home."

He reached to touch Socks's neck. "You recognize it, boy? When you left, you were a young horse, no more than five or six. Now you're getting old, but here you are again."

The gelding threw up his head and whinnied loudly. From down the track there came another whinny, and a horse came jogging into view.

"Gene?" yelled Cleve. "I'm back!"

The rider had pulled up and stared at them as if stunned. In a moment the man came toward them again, sweeping his hat from his crop of yellow hair. "Cleve? I'm not Gene, I'm Tim. Your baby brother! By gum, it's plumb good to see you, even if you do look like an Injun. Where in hell did you come from?"

"Better not let Ma hear you talk like that," Billy Wolf's father replied. He nudged Socks forward beside the piebald mare his brother rode and reached to give the young man a bear hug.

Then he drew back and gestured for the boy to come even with them. "Meet your nephew Billy Wolf. I brought him back because I had a feeling the folks might not live too much longer. I wanted him to know his kin."

Although his voice hadn't changed, the boy felt his father grow tense as he asked, "Pa? He's still alive, I take it?"

Billy Wolf stared up into pale eyes, much like his father's but not so sky-colored. His uncle nodded. "Pa's alive. He's not the man you recall, Cleve. Not by a long shot. He can't hurt anybody now. But I'll wait and let you see for yourself."

This new uncle looked down at the boy and smiled. "Glad to have a nephew. Gene's all broke out with girls, seems like. You'll likely liven 'em up a bit. Ma's got 'em so ladylike I can hardly stand 'em."

"You haven't any of your own?" Cleve asked.

"Not me. I've got to stay home and look after the folks. No girl I've met so far wants to take on a husband and his parents both, though I haven't quit looking."

They turned together and rode along the sandy road, Cleve and his brother talking about the crops, the cattle, the farm. The boy wondered where this keen interest in such white man's things had hidden while his father trapped and hunted and rode the mountains. He had never guessed that part of Cleve Bennett existed.

When they had hitched the horses and gone through the gate amid a loud barking of dogs, Billy Wolf found himself looking into the eyes of a small woman so unlike his mother that he hardly knew her for a woman at all. She was dressed in pale cloth that flapped about her legs and ankles in loose folds; her hair was white, pinned tightly on top of her head. Her eyes snapped gray fire as they met his, and he knew instantly that this would be, if not an enemy, at least not any sort of friend. All his instincts told him that.

But the old man on the porch was another thing entirely. Cleve had never talked about his father, so Billy Wolf had no idea what sort of man he might be. Never had he expected someone so tall, so gaunt, so helpless as the pitiful hulk sitting in the chair.

Something inside the boy opened to him, and Billy Wolf felt no revulsion as the old man touched his face and tried to speak. There was a person trapped inside there, trying to communicate with him and unable to force a word from his lips. It gave the boy a feeling of desperation, thinking about what that must be like. His captivity among the Shinni was nothing compared with what his grandfather suffered.

How unlike Buffalo Horn this one was. Even after the raid, his Tsistsistas grandfather got about, spoke with keen intelligence, and did the things he was able to do with speed and determination.

This one seemed hardly able to stand. Indeed, his uncle held him by the arm, steadying his feeble steps as he guided him into the house, where the strange smells of white man's food filled the air.

This was not the sort of cooking smell the boy knew, but his mouth watered. He was not disappointed. Only after he had cleaned his portion did he look closely at the table. There were flowers on the pots, and he wondered how they had been put there. He felt himself smiling as he touched the slick surface.

He looked up to see his grandmother watching him. For once she did not look unhappy, and she almost smiled in return. Perhaps she would not be as hard to understand as he had thought. He wondered if she had been the one who painted this wonderful pot.

They finished the meal, and instead of going out beneath the trees and putting down their bedrolls, his father led him into the back of the cabin, where there was a small square room for them to sleep in. There they put their supplies, after handing over the bear meat and the hide to Tim and his mother. The other gifts waited for later.

The place smelled strange, musty and close. Billy Wolf sniffed. "It smells better outside," he observed.

"Never let Ma hear you say that!" his father replied. "She keeps a clean house, and it would kill her to think it smelled bad. But it does, after sleeping in the open. Even a tipi, full of smoke and cooking smells, is better than damp wood that's full of dry rot and old smoke."

"What will we do here?" the boy asked. "We came. Do we hunt for them or help them steal horses from other white men?"

Cleve fell flat on his buffalo robe and stifled his laughter. When he could speak, he said, "Believe it or not, white men don't steal horses. At least not so they admit it. And when horse thieves get caught, they're killed. No, my folks don't need hunting or raids. I think what they need is to know I'm alive and well, now that I'm here.

"We'll think what we can do tomorrow. Right now I'm full and tired and I'm going to sleep."

Though he hadn't expected to sleep in this strange place and so near these newfound kin, Billy Wolf opened his eyes to dawn before he knew he had dozed off. A shrill cry from some large bird filled the air with its raucousness.

That woke Cleve, who put his arms behind his head and smiled. "Been a long old time since I woke to a rooster crowing," he said. "Tim's probably gone to milk, along about now, and Ma's stirring in the kitchen. Time to rise, my son, and see what today will bring. Besides our making tracks to Gene's. I can't wait to see that boy and his young'uns."

The boy, used to rising as soon as he woke, was already rolling up his sleeping robe. "Do they have a creek?" he asked his father. "I need to swim and get the dust off me."

"Sounds like a good idea," Cleve replied. "We'll slip out and have a dunk in the old swimming hole while Ma fixes breakfast. Time enough to pitch in and do the chores once we get all settled."

They returned from the creek, damp and spotless, to find Cleve's mother pink with her efforts over the iron stove. Slices of ham curled on a platter, and eggs, huge things unlike the bird eggs Billy Wolf was used to, had been scrambled into a fluffy heap. Slices of bread and butter were a revelation to the boy, and as he ate he wondered how it was possible for people to possess such a wealth of food.

But he said nothing. He was used to understanding the world around him, the ways people worked and acted and lived. This was alien to him, and he didn't want to seem ignorant. He decided to watch carefully, to remember everything he saw, and to ask his father privately about anything that puzzled him.

There was so much talk over the table that he had no chance to speak anyway. He listened hard to his uncle's words, trying to make sense of terms like *breeding stock* and *yearlings* and *new ground* and *haystacks*. It sounded as if being a white man must be terribly hard work. When did he hunt and fish and simply ride away to think?

After the meal Cleve gestured for the boy to follow and set off on foot along the pale sand of the road. The hot sun of summer had dried it quickly since the last rain, and they kicked up puffs of dust behind them as they moved. Bushes and trees crowded up to the track and leaned over it, so the boy felt as if he moved down one of the tunnels he had explored back in the mountains.

After a bit his father turned off the track and pushed through a thick hedge of wild rose, holding it back so Billy Wolf could get through without being too badly scratched. Beyond the tangle there was a space where all the prairie dogs in the world must have dug frantically, for the earth was damp and red brown, ridged in long furrows.

"What kind of an animal could do this?" he had begun to ask when he saw something moving in the distance. A horse. Yes. But it was not being ridden. Instead it was pulling some kind of travois that plowed into the soil, turning up fresh earth as it came.

As the horse pulled the thing closer Billy Wolf saw that a man walked behind, holding on to a pair of curved sticks. When he looked up from the turning soil and saw them standing beside the hedge, the man pulled on the lines to stop the animal.

"Whoa!" he yelled. "What on earth . . ." He came running clumsily through the loose dirt, his face red with heat and emotion. "Cleve? Dammit, Cleve, is that you?"

"Sure is, Gene." Cleve stepped forward and grabbed his brother around the shoulders. They danced in a circle, laughing aloud.

Billy Wolf had never seen his father behave so in his life; suddenly he wondered if there might be a bit of a boy still left inside the big man. This was the way he and the boys of the Tsistsistas had greeted each other on his return from his adventure.

The pair turned, shoulder to shoulder, and looked down from their great heights at him. Their faces were much alike, both reddened by weather and the heat, both blue-eyed topped with blond hair. It made the youngster feel dizzy for a moment to see two fathers standing there.

Snip, who had wagged along behind them on the walk from the house, had no such confusion. He knew the smell of his own man, and he moved past the boy and stood beside Cleve's foot, looking up inquiringly.

"And this is another Snip," Cleve said to his brother. "Old Snip saved my bacon more times than I can count, and he wound up dying to save the boy, here, and my wife. When we picked up this little fellow in the village, I was pleased when Billy Wolf wanted to name him for the old dog."

"We still have a Snip, too," Eugene said, bending to pat the dog's head. "Must be the great-great-grandson of the original dog. Maybe the boy would like to have another pup. Make a pair of 'em, and one will be the Snip bloodline, whatever that might be."

He seemed shy as he reached to take the boy's hand. "Mighty glad to know you, son. You go on down the road a piece and you can meet your cousins and my wife, Sarah. Come on. I got to see her face when I tell her my brother's come home again."

"What about the horse?" Billy Wolf asked, turning to look at the animal, which stood with one hind foot cocked, his eyes half-closed as if he took an opportunity to doze.

"Rufe'll stand there till dark if nobody bothers him. I can take off an hour to welcome home my long-lost brother, come hell or high water. Come on here, son, and let me lift you over this tangle." The big fellow swooped down and swung Billy Wolf high, setting him down in the track again.

The three went down the shaded road, Snip dotting a network of pawprints into the sand as if knotting their tracks together. They went around four bends before a chorus of yelps and deep barks sent the pup to Billy Wolf's side for protection.

"Sarah!" Eugene yelled. "Come see who's here!"

Two pale-haired children came running around the house, their limp skirts flapping around skinny legs. Billy Wolf stared blankly at the pair, for their faces were as pale as milk, spotted with reddish-brown blotches. Never in his life had he seen anyone with a spotted face.

Then he heard a voice that sent a chill up his spine. It was like a song or a chant, its tones soothing and quiet. The woman who spoke stood on the porch, drying her hands on her apron, looking down with surprise at her unexpected visitors.

"My brother Cleve, Sarah! I never thought we'd see him again. And his boy, Billy. They came in yesterday evening and I never knew a thing about it till they sprouted up at the end of my row, big as life. You got the kettle on? We'll have some mint tea, maybe." He turned and grimaced. "Been out of coffee for a while now. Money's been tight."

Billy Wolf looked sideways at the two little girls, who were looking sideways at him. Their fingers twisted bits of the cloth of their skirts, and their mouths were open with astonishment.

"He's an Injun," the taller one said at last, in a voice so quiet her father just caught it.

Cleve smiled, but his eyes were alert. "His mother is a

warrior of the Cheyenne. We were married by a Methodist preacher. He's half-Indian and half-Scotch-Irish."

"As if that made any difference," Sarah caroled. "You come right in here and sit down. I made a molasses cake yesterday, and I've got apple cider cool in the spring house. We don't find new relatives often enough to waste the chance to sit down and get to know each other."

Billy Wolf stared into the fair face. She was unlike his other kindred, being red of hair and cornflower blue of eyes, but there was something about her that felt like his own mother. Something strong and straight and not apt to get upset over trifles.

He smiled up at her and held out his hand. She reached down and hauled him onto the porch. Without any fuss, she swept the entire group, except Snip, into the kitchen and settled them at the long board table.

For the first time since leaving his mother's tipi, Billy Wolf felt entirely at ease and at home. His grandmother made him wary. His grandfather filled him with pity. His other uncle was fine, but this one and his wife were of the same sort of tribe as his Tsistsistas people.

His eyes met his father's across the table. Cleve grinned as if reading the boy's mind. With sudden clearness, Billy Wolf knew that his father felt the same.

Unexpectedly the boy felt a twinge of sadness. He would have liked, he realized, to feel this way about that other family up the road, but it was impossible. He knew he never would.

chapter

— 11 —

It was strange, being home again. Always, when he was a youngster, Cleve had been afraid, either of his father or of the God his mother feared. There had always been a watchful eye, belonging to one or the other, peering over his shoulders and examining everything he did.

He hadn't known it at the time, but now Cleve understood what a great weight he had abandoned when he left the farm and the Missouri country behind him. Danger was no burden—it was a matter of course out in the wild country to which he had traveled. Death was no punishment, merely the consequence of mischance or sickness.

He hadn't had the time to think about that much until his encounter with a buffalo bull on a certain frosty morning during his first winter away from home. That wicked red eye, the silver-frosted coat, the perilous horns had frightened him into believing in the devil for a very long while.

It was the Cheyenne who had given him a different idea of life and death. Guilt was no part of their way; their lives were harsh enough without that to add fear to their burdens.

He had found, as the years passed, that other tribes lacked that focus on guilt as well. Only the whites, locked into the old cultures that produced them, clung to the notion with desperate intensity, comparing themselves, when drunk, to lowly worms and miserable sinners. When they were drunk, they were both of those, of course, but most of those men were brave and fairly honest people as they went about their daily lives. The groveling did nothing but make them miserable.

The change had come to him suddenly as he adapted to his new life. Second Son had been of great help in that, and now that he was in his mother's house again, Cleve understood that he must walk very warily. If Mattie Bennett realized he no longer shivered before her strait-laced God or feared His irrational anger, she would be both furious and devastated. And she would blame his unseen wife for his defection.

So as the days passed and he and Billy Wolf helped about the place, shoring up snake-fenced patches of melons or corn with saplings cut from the wood or helping to rake and stack the hay in the river meadows, he watched his tongue. The boy was under enough pressure from his grandmother. He didn't need any more caused by his father.

Mattie seemed intent upon catching the child out in some unforgivable lapse of manners or morals. At last, one hot July morning, it all came to the surface, and there was nothing Cleve could do to stop it.

The corn was tall in the fields, the hay stacked until another cutting. There was nothing much to do except sit on the porch and mend harness and boots and clothing while talking idly.

Billy Wolf had been wrestling amid a tangle of obstreperous dogs, who had licked him from head to heels. When he surfaced, breathless and giggling, he washed himself in the water kept handy in a bucket on the porch.

Then he looked up at Cleve. "Can I go to see Lissa and Maybelle?" he asked. "There's nothing else to do. I could take a watermelon and we could sit in the shade and eat it."

"Sounds like a good notion to me," Cleve answered. "We have a little one you could carry over there; it's keeping cool under the chinaberry tree. Tell Sarah and the girls hello for me."

"I don't think that's such a good idea," Mattie said, her tone quiet but sharp. Her hands, busy shelling peas in the pan in her lap, went still and the knuckles whitened on the hulls she held.

Cleve, for the first time in his life, looked at his mother with dislike. He knew what she felt about the boy, but that was no reason to put a distance between him and his cousins.

He nodded again. "You go right along, son. Be back before dusk, though. Snakes are moving around in this heat."

Billy Wolf caught up the melon, which was awkward to carry but not too heavy, and headed down the road, disappearing behind the hedge of roses and creepers and honeysuckle vine. Only when he was out of hearing, which Cleve knew because he could no longer hear Snip's excited yips as he followed the boy, did he turn to look at his mother.

"Ma, I know you don't like it I married a Cheyenne. I know you wanted another towheaded grandchild. But Billy is a good boy, as good as they come. He's bright and quick and strong and honest. You can't deny he's been as much help as any man, since we came."

Mattie sent a hail of peas into the pan, rattling loudly as they hit. "I know he's the child of a red-skinned woman who's no Christian. Indian women are all whores. My own cousin told me that, years ago when he came to visit. How a son of mine could touch one, much less marry her!

"And that young limb of Satan is a savage. What will he do to those poor innocent little girls if he gets the chance? Even as young as he is, you never know what's in the mind of one of *them*. Sarah is too innocent herself to see the danger. You ought to see it yourself, Cleve, and do your best to stop it."

He stared at her, puzzling out her meaning from the flood of words. When he understood what she had said, he felt himself turn red with anger.

"You think that that little boy would *rape* Gene's girls?" he asked, trying to keep his voice down. "You mean that is actually what you think?"

"Of course. Everybody knows Indians carry off white women and make them into squaws. It's in his blood, son."

She looked straight into his eyes, and Cleve knew she was totally convinced of the truth of her words.

He drew a long breath, let it out slowly, and made himself as calm as possible. "Ma, some Indians are loose, like some white people. Some ain't. Cheyenne don't mess around before they marry. They don't mess around much even *after* they marry, because they limit their children. They wait, a lot of 'em, six or seven years between their babies.

"It was a long time after Billy Wolf was born before Second Son let me touch her again. She's a strong woman, and she controls everything she can about her life. What she can't control, she manages to endure, like we all have to. Her son's been taught since the day he was born to control himself.

"Lord, you know how she taught him not to cry when it might bring enemies down on us? She took his cradleboard and hung it in a bush, almost out of earshot from the tipi, and let him yell himself quiet. Took three times, and then he never cried again. He's got more control than any white *man* I ever met, and that's God's truth."

Seldom did Cleve talk so much. Never had he talked so to his mother. Now Mattie stared at him, her hands still, her eyes wide, but he could see that his words meant nothing to her. She had accepted the myths about Indians as totally as those the preacher taught her about God. She'd never change her mind, and that made him want to cry himself.

Cleve rose, hanging the cheekstrap he had been sewing to its buckle on a peg on the wall. "I better go see to the horses," he said. "Since it quit raining, the creek might be running dry."

Behind him there was a gasp of effort. Jase . . . he turned to see his father's pale eyes, wide with meaning, staring up at him. The thin hand moved to touch his knee.

Mattie glanced from one to the other, her eyes narrowing as she tried to interpret this unusual activity in her passive husband. But Cleve ignored her and reached down to take Jase's hand.

"You want to come walk with me?" he asked. "I think you can make it out to the horse pasture. The ground's pretty smooth and I don't think it'll trip you up."

Jase nodded and struggled to rise. Even with his son's help it was hard for him, but he made it upright at last. Cleve put his arm around his father, holding him under the shoulders, and half carried him down the steps. Once on level ground the old man seemed steadier, and he gave a shrug that told his son he needed no more assistance.

Cleve felt strange helping Jase that way. Not since he was a child, before Tim's birth had turned his father sour and angry, had he touched or been touched by this man in anything other than anger, with the intent to hurt. He had dismissed all his memories of his father as too painful to hold on to, but now he had the odd sensation that everything was about to change forever.

Despite the shade of the big oaks and elms and hickories, it was hot. The sun beat down on the crowns of the trees high above them, and its heat seemed trapped beneath the branches. Cleve sweated freely as he moved beside Jase, keeping his steps slow and glancing aside from time to time to see if there was anything his father needed.

What had been in the old man's mind? He couldn't speak, that was sure, and he never had learned to read and write. How could he communicate whatever it was that he wanted to tell his son?

In silence they moved through a web of birdcalls, distant bellows from a lovesick bull, the screeching of insects, and the occasional flutter of breeze among the leaves. The gate into the horse pasture was set beneath a tremendous ash tree, whose bole formed one of the anchoring posts; when they arrived there, Cleve leaned on the top plank, waiting for his father to do whatever it was he had come to accomplish.

Jase reached into his pocket and took out a slim bit of lead. Cleve recognized one of his mother's homemade pencils, formed by pouring melted bullet lead into a grooved plank and letting it harden.

Even as he wondered what his father could do with it, Jase marked on the gate plank, *Can rite now. Lissend to Mat tch grls.*

Cleve straightened, feeling a sudden excitement. "Does Ma know?" he asked. Surely she had been excited at having her husband become suddenly literate!

The veined hand was writing again: *No. Kep sekrit. Mat don't want me to. I dun her rong all them yrs. Now she got me bak.*

Cleve felt a fist clench around his gut. Was it possible that his mother, who had flung her frail body between him and his father's brutal fist so many times in his youth, had become as cruel in her turn as Jase?

"Is she mean to you?" he asked, his voice almost choked to a whisper.

The hand moved as quickly as it could manage. *No. No. Not mean. She don lissen.*

And there, Cleve thought, he had it. His mother, warped by those years of pain and humiliation, had enclosed herself like a turtle, keeping out whatever was most hurtful. Nothing she didn't want to hear could get to her anymore. Not Jase. Not Billy. Not Cleve himself.

He felt a wave of pity pass through him. What a skimpy life she led, this woman who had been so warm and filled with joy when her sons were tiny. What a terrible burden of guilt Jase's mother bore for turning him against his innocent wife and even more innocent youngest son.

Suddenly Cleve desperately wanted to believe in the burning hot hell his mother's preachers had always taught. He wanted to think that his grandmother Bennett turned on a spit over a particularly white-hot coal bed, her spiteful juices sizzling into the flames.

"What did you want to tell me, Pa?" he asked, trying to push away that nasty vision. It was unworthy of his new self and his new family back in the plains.

Tak boy. Go hom. She nevr lik him. Mite hurt him. Mat's not the womn you new. Gets funny somtims. I kin tell you groad up good. Sory bout evthin. The hand wavered to a halt, and the pale eyes gazed into Cleve's earnestly.

A lump rose in his throat. This was the father who had tossed him high, as a baby, roaring with laughter and catching him in strong, sure hands. He put one hand over his father's fingers and squeezed. Then he took a clod of dirt and rubbed it over the straggling words, blotting them out; he would not have them haunt either of his parents after he was gone.

"I know, Pa. I figured that out this morning, after Billy Wolf left and Ma went so funny. I hate to—Tim and Gene and I like to work together and we just barely got caught up on things, but you're dead right. We've got to go home again."

Jase's lips shaped a question. "Waaa i li?"

"What's it like? It's the wildest country you ever dreamed of. The land and the sky come together so far off that you never get there till the mountains pin it down. That takes weeks of riding through grass so tall it comes near up to your shoulders when you're on a horse.

"It's clean and dry. The clouds rise up white and tall and sail across the sky, and anybody riding toward you starts as a little bitty speck and gets bigger and bigger as he comes into sight over the swells. But even when he's right there by you, he looks like an ant, because the country's so huge."

He glanced aside, surprised at his own eloquence. He hadn't known what a grasp the wide country had on his heart until he put it into words.

Again Jase's lips moved. "P'pl?"

"They're not like us. They every one go their own ways, and no man's a boss, not many tribes keep slaves. The women work hard and will fight if they need to. The men hunt and raid for horses and keep an eye on whoever is moving over the country. There's a lot of time just to ride and think and play jokes and do nothing much. It's not like farming at all."

He chuckled, thinking of the way he'd been taught to feel guilty about idle moments. "They sing a lot, too. Long chants that tell the story of the entire tribe since the year one, seems like sometimes."

Jase looked amazed. Cleve knew this was like nothing he had heard of Indians. He whistled for Socks, who came trotting to the fence, followed by Blaze and the packhorse. The farm horses, curious, tagged along after a time, and

Cleve stood beside his father, scratching foreheads and smoothing noses.

It had been good to come home again. Yet now he knew that his true home was back to the west, where the mountains pinned the endless grasslands to the endless sky.

chapter

— 12 —

The great summer hunt was over. The Burning Hearts had killed many buffalo, in company with the rest of the Tsistsistas, and the racks were full of drying strips of meat. Robes were in all stages of treatment, and sinew, bone, and horn were being put to use. Not even the guts of the great beasts were wasted, for water and storage bags for pemmi-can were made of the cleaned intestines and stomach.

Second Son had killed four herself, lacking only one of equaling her brother's and her nephew's tallies. She had ridden on two long scouts to make certain the Comanche had not returned to the hunting grounds of her people.

She talked long with the other warriors in the evenings, when the wind was cool from the west and the fires flickered in its gusts.

But there was a great lack in her life. She had not known that she was alone before she and Yellow Hair became mates, but now his absence was a painful throb that permeated everything she did. Her son's absence left an even greater space in her heart, which seemed empty and waiting.

She often scanned the wide stretches to the east, hoping to see a pair of heads, one blond, one darker but with bright glints in the sunlight, appearing and disappearing as their owners moved up and down the swells of grassland. But they did not come.

Midsummer was past, and the dry weather had turned the prairie tan and gold. The Burning Hearts moved back toward the mountains, keeping well south of the Sioux lands around the Bad Gods' Tower. When the pale shimmer of distant peaks drew near, they found a well-watered place at the edge of the foothills and camped there.

That seemed to take her even farther from her family, and she knew it would be hard for Yellow Hair to find this new site for the village if he came after the signs of their passing had weathered away. At long intervals as the band moved, Second Son placed signs that only the two of them understood; she arranged rocks in patterns that seemed natural but were not to a knowing eye. Branches broken by wind were twisted slightly out of position, revealing paler wood. Cleve's quick eye would catch everything, she knew.

He would know that it was her hand that guided him toward his people again. But inside her was a deeply hidden fear. Would he, finding his own kind again, become one of them and stay in his home country with their son? Must she return to her solitary life?

Second Son did not allow that thought to reach the surface of her mind. Instead she pushed herself harder, now that they were near the mountain haunts of deer and beaver. She rode alone to hunt in the high country, sometimes absenting herself for days at a time and returning not only with meat but with plants—roots and leaves and seeds that had medicinal uses.

Sitting in the tipi of her brother while her sisters-in-law sorted through her newest contribution of herbs, she ventured to mention a recent concern to Singing Wolf. Their father dozed beyond the fire, and she spoke quietly to keep from waking him.

"I had a dream, brother. Three times it has visited me in sleep, and three times I have waked, ready to call out and warn our people. Yet it is not, I think, a danger to us. I believe it to be a danger to my own family."

Singing Wolf turned dark eyes toward her, his lean face attentive. "Your dreams have been valid, my brother. What was this one?"

"I saw riders, very distant on the plain. Clouds towered over them as if to crush them, and rain poured as if to drown them. But ahead of them the dry grass waved, and they rode hard to get out of the storm.

"As they reached the dry ground the fire-from-the-sky forked down before them, and where it licked the earth, smoke began to rise. Before they could see that the grass was ablaze, it was running even into the places where rain had fallen, so hot were the flames." She gazed into the fire, avoiding her brother's gaze.

"I rode hard, shouting a warning, trying to find a way to protect them, but I was too far away. When I came to the place where the fire had begun, there was a wide space of gray ash stretching in all directions, altogether lifeless and barren.

"I pulled my horse to a halt. Raising my voice, I sang loudly, calling to those who had ridden there to return, for the fire was gone." Her heart chilled as she remembered the dream. "And two gray shapes, one large and one small, rose up from the ash before me and stared at me with hollow eyes while the wind curled the ash about us all."

She looked up at last to meet Singing Wolf's gaze. He looked grim; his mouth hooked down and his eyes narrowed. This peace chief was also a dreamer of dreams, and often these had given hope and help to their people. He knew, if anyone did, how to interpret such a vision.

"This is a strong dream, my brother. I must think of it for a time. I will talk with the old men as well, for they have long experience of dreaming. But I will tell you that I believe this does not mean that your people must die.

"Tomorrow I will tell you more. Go now to rest, for the sun is down. The wind grows cooler from the mountains, and soon the leaves will fall. Think of that and sleep peacefully," he said.

She trusted Singing Wolf as she did herself. So Second Son went to her empty tipi and rolled herself into her sleeping robe. As if speaking of the dream had given her respite, she slept dreamlessly until morning, when she woke more hopeful than she had been for many days.

She did not shirk her tasks. She rode with the young warriors into the plain to scout for intruders. She sat with her nephew as he asked her innumerable questions about the ways in which Yellow Hair trained animals to do as he told them. She fletched new arrows to replace those lost in her last hunt.

Only when the sun was almost touching the tops of the mountains did she go again to her brother's tipi, where her father dozed by the fire and her busy sisters-in-law made her welcome. Soon Singing Wolf came in from his own tasks and sat across from her.

They drank broth from horn cups and then dug into the pot of dogmeat stew. Bread made from stored grass seeds finished their meal, and only then did they begin to speak.

"I have talked with the elders and with our father, who does not sleep as much as he appears to. Their opinions are my own. We think this is a warning. We think you should ride eastward, along the track they took when they left us. Yellow Hair and your son will face danger.

"It may be that you can save them or help them to save themselves. The season has come when only the women and children need to labor, gathering nuts and seeds for winter stores. Warriors sit idle, much of the time. For that reason we believe that my son Rakes the Sky with Lightning should go with you. Two are better than one when faced with unknown perils."

Second Son felt a lightening about her heart. She would go, and Cub would go with her. Perhaps together they could help her people as they returned westward. It was not until later that she realized that her dream also meant Cleve and Billy Wolf were, indeed, coming home again to the Tsistsistas.

Then she felt stronger than she had in many weeks. When she and her nephew set out toward the rising sun, she knew that she could battle storms and lightning, if necessary, in defense of those who were so dear to her.

They rode without haste, for the horses must last; there was no possibility of replacing one that broke a leg in a prairie-dog hole or was overridden to the point of death. She felt in her bones that the dream meant she would be in time to help her family, without desperate hurry. As if drawn by an invisible thread, she led her nephew toward the south and east, in the direction Cleve had marked into the dirt as he talked of his trip homeward.

They crossed the river the white men called the Platte and still headed toward the southeast. In time, tall clouds assaulted them with wind and rain, breaking the drought, and the dry washes they crossed filled with water. But she was on her way, and that was enough.

"The sky is dark," Lightning said one afternoon as the horses plodded along, heads down, weary with a long day of moving through the grassy tangles. "I think there will be another storm soon. I feel a tingle in my skin."

Second Son had been noting the thick line of darkness that was bearing down from the northwest. The day had been muggy, with a damper heat than usual, and she knew from old experience that sometimes devil winds descended in such weather.

"There may be broken ground ahead," she said. "I do not like to be riding on the flat land when it storms. Lightning and wind have slain our people more than once when they have remained unsheltered."

They urged the horses forward, leaning over their necks and peering into the increasing murk for the line of trees that might mark a creek. Behind them rumbles of thunder began to shake the sky, and their horses, though weary, picked up their pace. They, too, feared the weather.

The sky grew darker, and the wind began to blow even harder, whipping the grasses and sweeping up dust and grit to swirl into their eyes. Then, to the south, Second Son spotted a dark line. Trees or rocks, it made no difference. Any shelter from the missiles driven by the wind was necessary.

As they pounded near, the noise of hoofbeats almost drowned by the roar of the wind, she saw that this was a rock-topped ridge whose plates of stone slanted, some broken, some whole, in many directions. Without slowing, she turned her stallion to pass the tall stone at the near end. Once they were sheltered behind the bulwark of rock it flanked, she could hear the whistle of wind between the toothlike broken slabs.

She dropped from her horse and led him forward, hearing Lightning's sorrel moving behind her. If they were lucky, this would be shelter enough.

She worked her way between leaning masses, leading her stallion deeper and deeper into the maze. When they arrived at a sheer wall against which bastions of stone lay at angles, she looked back the way she had come. The place was like a forest, rising high overhead, impossible to see through because of the intricate jumble in which they stood.

Now the roar of the wind was so great that the ear refused to accommodate it. A fine mist of dust filled the air and the horses backed their ears and buried their noses against the rock. Second Son followed suit, laying her arm against the wall and thrusting her nose into the curve of her elbow.

A great shriek of sound tore the sky, and she knew that the black belly of the devil wind must be passing over them, for there was a sudden feeling of emptiness and her ears popped. Then the tension eased, and she ventured a glance at the sky.

Rain flooded down in streams from utter darkness. No trace of sky or cloud was visible. The world was all black water, falling so hard that it was almost as if it fell upward as well as down.

She drew a shuddering breath, feeling as if she had been holding it for hours instead of minutes. The noise had dwindled to the pounding of rain on rock, and now she heard the nervous whickers of the horses and the grating of their hooves on the gravelly soil beneath.

A hand touched her shoulder. "There is shelter here," said Lightning. "Perhaps we should camp, even though it is early yet. Sometimes these storms come together, and another devil wind might dance up from the southwest when we gain the open country again."

That was good thinking. Even if Cleve and Billy Wolf were traveling westward, they would surely have taken cover from such weather. She grunted assent and gentled Shadow when she tried to rear and snort before moving into the tangle of rocks again.

A fire would be well hidden here, and its warmth would dry their clothing and moccasins. It was best to remain in shelter when storms tore across the plains country. Tomorrow they would be off again, heading toward the place where her heart told her she might find her husband and son.

chapter
— 13 —

When Billy Wolf returned, before dark as he had been
asked to do, Cleve found himself ready to begin saying his
good-byes to brothers and parents. He had learned a great
deal about both Jase and Mattie, none of it anything like
his preconceptions. He had re-formed his bonds with both
brothers. Now it was time to go home again.

"We're going back west," he told his son as they washed
up in the wooden bucket on the porch. "You ready to see
your mother again, and your Cheyenne kin?"

The dark eyes turned toward him, and a light dawned
behind them. For the first time Cleve realized that, young

as he was, the boy had felt his grandmother's revulsion every time she looked at his aquiline features and Indian eyes. He'd thought only the adults understood her feelings about this half-Indian grandson, but now he knew he had been wrong.

"I'll miss the girls and the uncles and Aunt Sarah," said Billy Wolf. "And my grandfather, I think, even if we can't talk much."

Cleve stared down at the thin brown shape of his child, noting with dismay how quickly he was growing. Where was the chubby baby he and Second Son had taken such delight in caring for? Had Jase felt the same about him and Gene as they shot up into manhood? And if so, how had he managed to forget the urgent fondness of father for son in order to abuse his children?

The boy moved toward his bedroll, his wiry shape graceful and economical in its motions. Cleve wondered again how anyone, even one so set in her ways as his mother, could fail to find the child lovable.

Though the Tsistsistas seldom spoke of their feelings for one another, they loved deeply. His wife and his brother-in-law felt for him, he knew, the emotions he held for them, though seldom was anything said about it.

His son sniffed. "She has cooked," he said. "It is good to eat many times in the day, but I would not like to work so hard in the fields, without time to ride or hunt, in order to make all that food."

Thinking about it, Cleve agreed. Comparing the life he had led here in Missouri to that experienced in the plains and the mountains, he found he much preferred the wild ways to the tame ones. Constant danger and hardship were the price of freedom, he had learned, but those were prices that did not seem too high for him to pay.

He said nothing to his parents or Tim as they ate breakfast. He felt there would be an emotional scene once his mother knew they were leaving, and he had always had a horror of those. Second Son had spoiled him for weeping women.

He sat for a time with his father on the porch, watching the sun filter through the leaves, the breeze stir eddies of dust in the scraped yard, while the dogs scratched fleas and sighed with boredom, their broad heads flopped onto their paws.

Billy Wolf sat in the shade, his back against the chinaberry tree's smooth dark skin. Snip curled at his side, his skinny tail whipping against the sand from time to time when the boy scratched his ears or laid a hand on his head. The pup from the old Snip's line lay in his lap.

So far the two animals had shown no jealousy, and Cleve hoped they were capable of becoming friends. A single dog had proven to be invaluable to him and his family. Two, well trained and cooperative, could become even more of an asset.

His father sighed deeply and put a frail hand on his arm. Cleve turned and looked into those faded eyes, trying his best to read what Jase might mean. It must be hard for Ma to figure out what he needed from such subtle signs.

The old man looked sadder than usual, and he patted his son's arm three times, in measured rhythm, as if saying good-bye. Was it possible he had understood what Cleve meant to do so quickly after the decision was made?

"I'm glad, Pa, that we've come to know each other better," he said. The eyes brightened just a bit. "We knocked heads pretty bad, back in the old days, but now I think we're friends, maybe. You know we're goin' soon?"

Jase nodded. His mouth worked, but nothing came out. His lips shaped the word *boy*.

"The boy? He's a good'un, isn't he? Smart and strong. I only wish Ma felt the same about him as you do. Too bad."

Jase nodded. Again he patted Cleve's arm. Then he pointed toward the road and gestured toward Gene's house, invisible behind the intervening mile of trees and bushes along the winding track.

Cleve smiled. "We're goin', in just a bit. I wanted to sit here and smell the flowers on Ma's rose vines and four o'clocks, the dust and the green leaves.

"The Absarokas're great mountains, with forests that run straight up and down the slopes. You can stand at the foot of one tree with the top of another in spitting distance. It smells high and clean and wild. But Missouri has its own smells, and I'm kind of storing them up to remember when I'm way off again."

He stood and Billy Wolf rose, too. Jase sighed again, this time with frustration, Cleve was sure, but he made no move as they ambled through the gate and out into the little road. Turning to raise his hand to his father, he saw that the old man had leaned forward in his chair as if trying to stay as close to them as possible.

The smothery scents of late-summer flowers filled the air, and the two pups ran in circles, stirring up the pale dust to mingle its acrid scent with that of growing things. A red fox darted across the road ahead of them, and Snip went yipping after it, while the smaller dog trailed him, tongue lolling, saying nothing.

"He trails quiet. Usually that means a good dog, lots of sense. We'll see. I'm glad to have the old dog's kin again. What you going to call him?"

Billy Wolf gave a crow call, and both dogs crashed through the bushes along the road, heading for his heels. "I think I'll call him Jase. After my grandfather." The dark eyes slid sideways, watching his father's reaction.

Cleve hid a smile. "Sounds like a first-class name to me. And Pa'll be mightily pleased, I suspect."

The boy set off at a run, the dogs behind him, toward the bend that marked the gate to Gene's house. Cleve heard the clamor of his brother's dogs as they greeted the newcomers.

Sarah's clear voice called, "Down! Down!"

Two shrill cries told him the girls had seen their cousin's arrival, and he moved more quickly to the gate and into the yard. He looked up at Sarah, who stood on the porch, her hair a blaze of auburn in the morning sunlight.

"Gene in the west field? Or has he gone to check on the cattle?" he asked his sister-in-law.

"He's gone to look for old Belle. She's got a new calf, most likely. It's her time, and she didn't come up this morning. The others have been grazing along the east pastures on the river. Why don't you go and see if you can find him while Billy plays with my girls?"

Cleve nodded. "I'll do that. We're about to set off again for the big country, Sarah, and I wanted to say good-bye. It's been good to be home, but it's time to go."

She looked a bit startled. "So soon? Seems like you just got here. Gene's been as cheerful, since you came, as I've ever seen him. He worries, that man, about his folks. He feels bad that Tim has the whole responsibility, too.

"That boy is too close to home. He's old enough to start a family of his own, and he never has time to get off and meet young ladies. We can see that he's been restless and unhappy lately."

"I've thought about that," Cleve said. "But if I've learned anything in the years I've been gone, it's that things will work out, one way or another. Tim will be all right. What bothers me is my boy. Ma just doesn't warm up to him, and he knows it. I think it's time to take him back home to his mother."

She nodded. "I've seen. The few times we've come up there since you came, I could feel Miz Bennett being bothered about him ... and his mother. That's the sticking point with her. She seems to have a real hate for all Indians, and she can't reconcile your boy, polite and disciplined and responsible, with what she's been told about the red-skinned people. It's mighty hard for an old person to let go of the things she's believed all her life.

"No, I understand your reasons. I just hate for you to go before she comes around. She's going to regret it once she realizes she'll never see either of you again."

Cleve smiled and turned into the woods, moving through the greenery, feeling spiderwebs, still damp with dew in the shade, sprangle across his face. The cow trail bore the prints of Gene's boots, and he followed them as they took a bypath toward the woods along the river.

A jaybird shrieked, high in an oak tree. A crow cawed a warning, and from far ahead another answered it. The shade was cool, but when he emerged into a pasture he had helped clear as a boy, the sun struck him like a hammer. At the other edge he could see movement, and Gene came into view, driving a cow ahead of him.

Old Belle's calf moved at her side, still dampish from being born. Cleve made a circuit to avoid spooking the cow as he approached his brother.

"Morning," he called.

Eugene grinned. "Got a brand-new heifer this morning," he called. "You going to help me drive 'em in?"

"Sure. But I wanted to say good-bye, too. The boy and me, we figure to start back west in a day or two. I haven't told Ma, but Pa knew, somehow."

Before Gene could answer, there came a distant roar that could only be a gunshot. The brothers stared for a split second in grim speculation. Then, forgetting the cow and the calf, they sprinted toward the wood and the house. Any gunshot had to be investigated at once, for varmints came in all sizes and either two- or four-footed shapes.

The wood flashed past as Cleve ran, and he came within sight of the house quickly. He paused; Gene came up beside him and laid a hand on his shoulder. He jerked his chin sideways, and Cleve understood.

They shouldn't go busting out into whatever was happening. If there were enemies at the house, getting blasted wasn't going to help.

They emerged into Sarah's garden and made their way up the path alongside the chinked log wall. Cleve peered around the corner into the front yard. Two men stood just inside the gate, their hands in the air. They were dirty, their beards filthy and uncombed, their rough clothing showing signs of long wear.

Gene slid backward and went into the house through the backdoor. Cleve took his knife out of his belt and held it ready in his hand. Someone was holding those men at gunpoint, and it had to be Sarah. As intently as he looked, he couldn't see the children.

Sarah's clear voice said, "That's right. Hold it tight so the blood can't come through. Your papa is coming right now, I know. He had to hear the shot. Just hold on, Lissa. We'll be fine when the men come."

Cleve eased around the corner just as Eugene came out on the porch to stand beside his wife. He had a flintlock, primed and ready, in his hands. Sarah held an ancient musket, and her hands were steady as she kept it aimed at the two in her front yard.

"What happened?" Cleve asked, keeping his voice calm.

"Look to your boy. These ... men ... shot him," she said, through gritted teeth. "They're only lucky that I didn't kill them both. If I hadn't had to reload, I would have taken one down, but I thought it was best to keep them here until you came."

But Cleve wasn't listening. He glanced around the yard and found a huddle of children beneath a bridal-wreath bush. Lissa, the older girl, was holding a wad of cloth tightly against Billy Wolf's upper arm, between the arm and his chest, but a red stain was coming through already.

He knelt beside the boy and gently took the wadding from the child's hand. "Let me see," he said.

Billy Wolf nodded. He was pale; his jaw was set and there was no sign of fear in his steady gaze, though pain had lined his young face. Cleve had seen his nephew Lightning look just that way, more than once.

A rifle ball had gone through the inner part of his upper arm, cutting a groove in the arm and scoring the skin of his side. Whoever had fired that shot intended to kill, and only luck had intervened. The boy must have moved just as the man fired at his chest.

Cleve held the stained cloth up and noted that it was a part of Lissa's dress, ripped hastily off one side of her ample skirt. He tore off a strip and bound it tightly around his son's arm to close the wound. Rolling another batch, he packed it into the streak along the boy's side and bound it in place with another strip. To his great relief, the flow of blood slowed, and the cloth stained only very gradually.

When he turned, he found the men still standing, but now Gene held his gun on them while Sarah had their rifles and knives in a pile beside the porch.

"These skunks tried to kill your son," Gene said. "You want to shoot 'em, or shall I?"

Cleve felt anger that surpassed even the fury he had felt years ago when Jase turned his whip against Mama. Killing wasn't in it—he wanted to take these bastards apart with his bare hands. He wanted to see the color of their blood and brains and guts decorating Sarah's tidy yard.

"You keep the other one from interfering. I want to put my hands on the one that did the shooting. Which one of you is that?"

He aimed the question like a bullet, and the taller of the men turned to look at him. "You the squaw man what brung this Injun brat to mess with white girls? You're the one ought to be kilt. He had his *hands* on that young'un!" The man's voice was filled with loathing and contempt.

"He was tickling my daughter, who had just tickled him," said Sarah. "This is our nephew, and you'd better be glad I took a minute to think, or one of you would be dead."

Cleve moved toward the man, who lowered his head,

bared his teeth, and charged like a bull buffalo. They came together like two mountain rams, the impact of their bodies almost knocking the breath from both.

But Cleve had fought hand to hand with mountain men. No backwoods farmer was going to best him, he felt with ferocious certainty, no matter how strong and heavy he might be. There were tricks to that game, and he had learned them in a harsh school in which death was the penalty for the loser.

He twisted sideways and rolled his adversary over his hip. The man hit with a thud, and dust flew. Then Cleve was on him, his teeth sunk in a filthy ear, his arms straining to crush the life from this would-be child killer clasped to his chest.

He felt sudden agony and knew that the man he held was biting his shoulder where it pressed against the bearded face. Setting his toes against the dirt, Cleve rolled them enough to dislodge the teeth, at the same time spitting out the half-moon of ear he had bitten off.

The man had found purchase evidently, for suddenly Cleve flew free and rolled to his feet, facing the bleeding farmer. He watched his eyes, and when the lunge came he was prepared for it.

Grunting, straining, he rolled about Sarah's neat yard, trying his best to find a way to break the wiry neck that seemed to slip out of his hand whenever he got a grip on it. Finally he found a chance and stood, hauling the man upright with both hands. He butted the grimy face full on with the top of his head. A crunch told him that the nose had broken, and the body he held went limp.

"Dirty Injun trick!" the other was saying when Cleve turned toward him.

But "That's enough!" came Sarah's voice from the porch. "I don't want murder done in my own yard and before the children. If you'd killed them right after they shot Billy, that would be one thing. This is another. Cool down, Cleve. Put the gun away, Gene. I think these men have had enough. I've sent Maybelle after Tim."

Cleve stood swaying, his heart racing, his fury beginning to dwindle. They were sorry specimens, it was true. Ignorant, dirty, full of venom—he'd met many of that kind in the wild country, and few of them survived even a year.

"You can handle it?" he asked his brother. "I want to get Billy back to Ma's. She's got a cure for anything known to man."

"Go," Gene answered. "We'll tend to these bastards. There's a marshal up to town, and that's where they'll end up, once we get a few neighbors to keep hold of 'em. I'll be up to see about the boy soon as we're done here."

Catching the boy carefully into his arms, Cleve turned and ran, followed by a pair of worried dogs. His first instinct was to turn to Ma, as it had been when he was Billy Wolf's size. He knew she would put aside her feelings once she saw the wounded child.

He thought with sudden longing of Second Son, calm and quick and full of knowledge of native cures. But Ma was good at that, too, and he ran even faster, with Snip yipping excitedly at his heels.

chapter
— 14 —

Jase had been restless all morning, getting up from his chair with great effort and standing at the edge of the porch while he stared down the road toward Eugene's place. Mattie kept only half her mind on her work, churning, working the butter, and setting the resultant pats, rounded off in a wooden bowl, to cool in a cedar bucket down the well.

It was hot. When she was done with butter making, she put on a clean apron and caught up a basket of runner beans to shell on the porch so she could keep an eye on her husband and get a bit of breeze at the same time. She was old enough so sitting down didn't come amiss; she sank into her splint chair with a sigh and took up a lapful of beans.

As they rattled into the pan she kept watching Jase. He paced the short length of the porch, each lagging step a separate frustration to both of them. He even started down the steps, holding on to the upright for stability, but she called his name sharply and he gave it up. It just wasn't safe, he was so unsteady on his feet.

The gunshot from down the road came as a shock. Few hunted in such hot weather, and somehow that sound had the ring of trouble in it.

Jase came to the chair and scrabbled at her shoulder with his thin fingers. "Go! Go!" his mouth shaped, though no voice added its weight to the word. "Boy!"

Cleve—had something happened to her son? She put the beans into the pan and stood, shaking her apron. Then she reached inside the house and grabbed the long gun she kept there for shooting varmints that got after her chickens. It was loaded, and all she had to do was prime the pan and check the flints once she got ready to shoot it.

"I'm going," she snapped as Jase tried to hurry her along. "You stay put, you hear me? Whatever happened, you can't do anything about it."

The words were cruel, and she knew that. She frequently said things to Jase that cut him deep, and it was on purpose more often than not. Sometimes her conscience kept her awake, thinking about that unchristian streak in her. But now she had no time to think about it. She hurried down the track, her weary feet and aching bones forgotten in anxiety about her son.

No further sounds of shooting came to her ears, and she

began to hope that Sarah had shot at a hawk circling over her chickens. But she kept on anyway, her gaze fixed always on the next bend in the twisting road.

When Cleve came into sight it was a shock, for he was running, the long lope of an animal bent on moving at speed for hours without stopping. She caught a sudden glimpse of the life he must have lived out there in the far mountains and plains, and it told her much about the perils he must have faced.

"Cleve!" she shouted. "You all right?"

His steps didn't slow until he came close. Then she saw that he held his son cradled against his shoulder. There was cloth wrapped about the boy's chest and arm, and the color of blood made a new pattern on the calico she knew so well, having made it up into the dress her granddaughter wore.

"Come!" She turned in her tracks, the gun now a hindrance, and sped back toward her own gate, her skirts flapping about her ankles, her aching joints forgotten in the urgency of the moment. She could hear Cleve's steps thudding behind her as she neared the porch.

Jase was waiting, bending forward in his chair, his face tense. He shifted as if to rise as she leaped up the steps, but she motioned him back down.

"Boy's shot," she gasped. "Be still! Work to do!"

She whisked the worn cover off the scrubbed wood of the kitchen table. The kettle, always filled and ready on the back of the stove, still held warm water, though the fire had been damped for hours. She poured a bowlful and grabbed a handful of lint from the bag she kept ready for accidents. In winter, while she sat beside the fire, she picked old cloth to bits, storing the fluff against the need to pack a wound. Clean rags were constantly at hand for such uses as well.

Cleve laid his son on the table and bent over him, his jaw set, his shoulders tight with anxiety. She laid her hand on his arm. "You go and sit down now. I know how to fix gunshot wounds, nobody better. The boy will sit still for me, won't you, William?"

Billy Wolf was pale under his coppery color. There were lines of pain around his mouth, but he was controlled, not whimpering as any other child she ever knew would have been.

He nodded, and Mattie knew that this was better than most people's sworn promises. Strange that she knew that so completely.

She cut the bindings and bared the twin grooves. When the strip of cloth came out, blood welled up, bright against the child's dark skin. The boy didn't flinch as she raised his arm, and his black eyes didn't allow a flicker of agony to show.

"Hold it right there," she said, and he nodded again, keeping the arm high enough to be out of her way. She dipped a soft cloth into the water and swabbed the wounds carefully. Already the blood was clotting, telling her that no major blood vessels were affected. But the tattered skin around the wounds was already fevered to her touch.

"He's getting feverish," she murmured. She raised her head and found Cleve leaning to see, his fingers obviously itching to help. "You go look in my pantry and find the pot of ointment, way at the back. It's in a jar with a lid, and it's marked 'Open Wounds.' I'll make some herb tea when the kettle boils."

Her son rose as if on springs and was off through the

backdoor to the small room at the end of the back porch
where she stored her herbs, medicines, and dried fruits and
vegetables. Relieved of his anxious attention, she quickly
cleaned the arm and the side and laid William back on the
table with a towel beneath his head. He closed his eyes,
and that was the only sign he gave that the movement had
been painful.

Cleve came, holding the jar, which was dwarfed in his
big hand. "This the one?" he asked, his tone reminding
her of the small boy he had been, often skinned or bruised
or suffering broken bones. How had he strayed so far from
her teachings?

She pushed the thought away as she smoothed the ill-
smelling gray ointment into blood-streaked grooves and
bound lint on top of it, tightly enough to slow the bleeding.
She felt a reluctant pride in William's stoicism. She had
heard that Indians didn't feel pain or emotion, but she
could see by the lines on the boy's face that he did, indeed,
suffer. He just didn't let it show, and such control was
something she could respect.

She motioned for him to lie still, and he relaxed, now
that the worst was over. Taking the washcloth, she gently
cleaned him from head to heels, removing the dust and
grit acquired from his morning of play and pain. To her
surprise, she found that his skin felt just like that of any
other child. It wasn't like touching a snake, as she had felt
it must be.

When she had him dried and wrapped in an old nightshirt that had been Tim's, she nodded to Cleve to lift him
off the table, led the way to the tiny back room where the
two slept, and unrolled the bedroll. When the boy was in

place, she smiled, the first unstrained smile she had given him since he arrived at her home.

"You rest now, William," she said. "If you need anything, just call. But it's best that you stay still. You lost a good bit of blood. Try to sleep."

The boy glanced at his father and Cleve nodded. The dark eyes closed as she turned from the room. After a moment Cleve came after her and led the way to the porch, looking pale and drained, and she understood at that moment how much of his heart was bound up in that half-Indian child.

Jase was waiting, his expression anxious. His lips formed the word *boy* again, the question plain on his face, and she went to stand beside him.

"William is resting. The wound was not serious, and he didn't lose too much blood, to judge by his color. I'll boil up some beef broth in a bit, and that should put heart into him. Don't worry yourself about him—he'll be just fine." She hoped her words would prove to be true, and if infection didn't set in, they should.

Jase's mouth was moving again. It looked as if he were saying "go" but surely that must be wrong.

"He can't go anywhere until he gets well!" she said. "You don't travel with a child who's been shot!"

Cleve dropped into the splint chair next to his father's and looked up at her. "We're going back, Ma. Soon. Maybe a couple of days."

"But the boy! What about him?" After seeing her son so concerned earlier, it was a shock to think he would take a wounded boy on the hard journey they would face. What sort of man had Cleve become, out there among primitive people and those who fled from civilized society into the terrible mountains and plains?

"He's Tsistsistas. He'll go without a whimper. And he won't get sick, either. He needs his mother, I think. I can see it in him, though he doesn't show it plain. He likes it here, but he's homesick. I've got to admit that I am, too. Missouri's not home anymore, though it was wonderful to see everyone again. Day after tomorrow, I expect we'll be on our way."

Mattie sank into her splint rocker and picked up the beans she had dumped so unceremoniously. Automatically her fingers began unzipping the hulls and raining beans into her pan. Was it her fault that her son wanted to go after only a few weeks back home? She had a disagreeable feeling it might be. She hadn't made his son welcome, that was certain.

But Mattie Bennett was a stiff-necked woman. The years since Jase lost the ability to harm her had made her even more hardheaded. So be it. If her son had married a heathen and was raising another heathen, that was on his head. She wouldn't accept any guilt in the matter.

Glancing up, she saw Jase's gaze fixed on her. He knew what she was thinking. More and more, since he had lost so much, he seemed to reach out with some inner sense and read the world around him.

His eyes were narrowed, as they did when he disapproved of what she was doing, and his fingers scrabbled against the knees of his breeches as if he might be trying to write. Which was nonsense. He never learned, and she had always held that against him, along with a lot of things less easy to forgive.

She looked down into the pan, now filling fast with

shelled beans. "I suppose if you must go, you must," she murmured, keeping her chin down to hide the angry crimp of her lips. "But we must have the family all together before you leave. Sarah and Gene and the girls must come to dinner on Sunday, after church. The circuit-rider preacher will be here this week."

It was Saturday, thanks be to God, so that left time to cook a big meal and get things ready. She was busy planning what to cook when Cleve interrupted her thoughts.

"Ma, I won't take the boy to church. He's not a Christian, and I think it might make him uncomfortable. His mother is teaching him the ways her people believe, and they work better out there in the far country."

She felt anger rise in her. She had raised a heathen! But she managed to control her tongue. "Why'd you trouble yourself to marry in the faith if you put no stock in it?" she asked.

"I didn't, really. Holy William was a Methodist preacher we rescued, and he was a friend. He trapped with us and at the end he saved my life. But before that, he was worried about Second Son and me living together and just being married the Cheyenne way.

"I hated to hurt his feelings. Besides, I know enough about my own kind to realize that if the boy has papers that make him legitimate, he's going to be better off, once a lot of whites move into the wild country and begin trying to set up their own ways." Cleve paused and stared down at his hands, which had unconsciously picked up a bit of harness that needed mending and were working away at it.

"It's a different world out there, Mama. You have to be careful about thinking you know the only right way. That can be dangerous, because there are people who live by their own right ways, and they get upset if you tell 'em they're damned and going to hell. Holy William found that out the hard way. I met the devil myself, up on the Missouri River, and he gave me a mighty tussle before I got on top of him."

Mattie pursed her lips. What nonsense was the boy talking? How had this Indian woman corrupted his mind and his morals? But she had the sense to keep her mouth shut. If they were going, she didn't want it to be with anger and harsh words.

After a moment she said, "Then I won't go either, though the preacher won't be around again for a month. We'll send Tim down to invite Gene's bunch and we'll start early."

Cleve, who had been looking apprehensive, sighed unconsciously with relief. She knew he had been dreading telling her that her own flesh and blood was an unbeliever, and she appreciated that. But it was no excuse for letting the boy remain outside the church.

Again she bit her tongue. Tomorrow would be a happy day, if there was any way on earth she could manage it. She would never see her son again, she knew. She would never see this wild grandson again, which was no hardship.

Tears came to her eyes, but she blinked them back. Life never was the way you expected it, and once she realized what Jase was, after Tim was born all those years ago, she should have stopped expecting anything at all.

chapter
— 15 —

Cleve had known it was going to be hard to leave; he had not forgotten his people and their needs, he found to his surprise, even after so many years of absence. Before going, he must entrust to someone the gold he had set aside for the family.

Every summer at Rendezvous he had made a habit of demanding coin for a set percentage of his plews. The money, safely stored beneath the bedding in the bear's den back in the Absarokas, was destined to help his son in the future. Second Son knew its location, as did her brother. She had approved his taking part of it to help his kin when they decided he must return to Missouri. Her people were not impressed by yellow metal.

He'd intended to hand it over to his mother, but now he realized that Mama was no longer stable, not quite capable of dealing rationally with such a sum. The gold half eagles, which traders preferred because they were lighter to transport than silver, had traveled all the way from the plains in a bag along with his extra moccasins and the lead for his seldom-used Hawken. He dug out the soft leather pouch and held it for a moment, thinking hard.

Pa couldn't handle it. Gene had enough to worry about, though he now knew the money was there if needed. Tim was the one to burden with the gold. He of them all seemed to require the security the money might mean for him and his parents.

The day had been busy, for Ma had the whole family there. The table groaned with food at midday, for Sarah brought her own contribution, as well as the girls and Gene. Talk went merrily around as they ate, and Cleve almost found it in him to be happy, though there was a dull weight of sadness deep inside.

Billy Wolf had slept the night through and he rose the next morning without complaint, even while his wounds were freshly dressed. Despite his grandmother's warnings about getting up so soon, the boy dressed in the outgrown pants and shirt that had been Tim's. He knew it would please Mattie to see him look "civilized." He moved with considerable ease, Cleve noted. They were a tough breed, the Tsistsistas.

Now everyone had left, after tight-lipped farewells and a few tears from Sarah and the girls. Mattie had whisked off to wash the dishes in order to avoid breaking down. She thought she'd fooled him, but Cleve knew his mother.

Jase was now abed, his snores vibrating through the house, and Mattie had joined him. Tim should be sitting on the porch in the cool of the night, resting and thinking over the day.

Cleve had seen his brother's sadness, and he knew he must go out and do this last thing for him. Tim had been given the rough end of the stick, from day one, it seemed. Now was the time to take at least a bit of the burden off him.

Nobody here had cash money. When wealthier people from the cities of the east started coming into the Missouri country's western lands, they were going to try their best to buy or finagle the rich bottomlands and the timbered high ground out of the hands of those who had wrested them from wilderness. This gold might well save the farm for his people, and if Tim knew he had it to draw on, if necessary, it might give him the slack he needed to go and find him a wife.

Just as Cleve expected, Tim had his long legs stretched out to the edge of the porch as he sat in Pa's chair. The back was tilted against the wall, and his head was leaned back, though it was too dark to see if his eyes were closed.

Cleve stepped out quietly and closed the wooden door behind him, though it shut off the breeze through the house. He wanted this conversation to be private.

"Tim, I've got something for you. Something Gene knows about, and I want you to give him access to it if he needs it." Cleve held the pouch between his hands, feeling the shift of coins under the leather.

The legs of the chair came to the floor with a soft thud.

"Cleve, I hate to see you go. It's been a lot easier, just knowing you were here. Pa's a handful sometimes, and Ma's getting to be almost as bad. She forgets and she frets and she drives me near crazy."

"I've got something that can help, if nothing but your feelings," Cleve said. He held out the bag, which clinked softly as he laid it in his brother's hand.

"There's a thousand dollars there, in gold half eagles. It's not all I've made, so don't worry about that. I've got at least that much more put by for the boy. I figure if you have some security laid up in a safe place, it'll give you a bit of breathing room.

"You go off to St. Louis or someplace and find you a girl and get married. Gene and Sarah want it for you, and so do I. You'll work yourself to death and never live at all if you keep on like you've been doing. I know—I didn't really live until I had a family of my own to work for.

"If Mama and Pa need something bad, dip into it. If not, just let it sit until there's a real problem that money can solve. You're goin' to need this, one day."

Tim took the bag, almost dropping it, for the gold pieces weighed heavy. Cleve heard him catch his breath with an incredulous gasp.

"Cleve, I . . . you sure you can afford to do this?" His voice was tight with excitement.

"Where I live you don't need money. What I've got put by is for the boy. Time'll come when money men come west. I can see it from what's happened here in Missouri. There's ten times as many people here as there were when I left, and more will come. And they won't stop at the Little Sac or the Missouri or the Platte. I can see white men breaking ground in the Black Hills one day.

"I want my son to have white men's weapons to defend himself when the time comes. Money is the best one I know."

His brother's shape was dark against the moon-spangled trees and the pale glimmer of dust in the yard. Tim sighed deeply and leaned the chair back again, the gold chinking in his lap. "You don't know what this'll do for me, Cleve. I been worried to death in case something comes along that takes money. We got about a hundred dollars saved up in all the time since you left.

"Horses sell all right, but time we get a pretty good bunch ready to go, the army stops buyin' or they get sick and we lose the best of 'em. Cattle sell slow and steady, but mostly for barter goods. I been too busy sweating to think about getting married. Now I can really get serious. I want young'uns before I'm too old."

Cleve smiled into the darkness. If nothing else, he had relieved his brother of a burden. Whether they knew it or not, his folks would be cared for more patiently than might otherwise be the case. He knew, none better, that a worried man tends to be fractious.

The next morning he and Billy Wolf were on the road before the sun came up over the treetops. Ma had insisted on cooking a big breakfast—ham and grits and rich milk and biscuits sopping with butter and honey from the wild bee tree the boys had found last spring.

Heavy with sadness and food, Cleve headed Socks for the ford and crossed the Little Sac, with Billy Wolf on Blaze just behind him. He felt that he would never cross the river, never see this rich country or his parents and brothers again.

The dusty shade was cool, in contrast to the staring sun, and he breathed deeply, setting the smell of home in his senses. He'd never come back. There was nothing for him there on the farm. His people had grown away from him as he'd grown away from them. He loved them still, but he no longer needed them.

No, he now longed for the clean winds knifing off snow-fields in the high reaches of the mountains or the tangy bluster of the prairie wind. He wanted to see Second Son's copper-skinned face relax one degree when she saw him. That was the equivalent, he now knew, of a white woman breaking into tears and flinging herself into his arms.

However, he wasn't going to hurry Billy Wolf. The boy said nothing, and Cleve knew he'd ride until he fell, if necessary, but there was no need.

So they meandered gently out of the hills and woods of western Missouri into the edge of the plains country, where oak scrub gave way at last to long swells of tall grass and occasional tree-lined creeks or small rivers.

He avoided notice if anyone appeared on the horizon. Those men his brother had turned over to the marshal back on the Little Sac had made threats and Gene had not failed to warn him. They were Tollivers, brothers from up on Horse Creek, members of a family that didn't know its own numbers.

"There's cousins and uncles and brothers and sisters and all kinds of kin scattered through the country. They're not bad people, but they are ignorant and vengeful, and if they follow up on what Lije and Carter threatened when the marshal took 'em away, you better keep a sharp eye out behind you," had been Gene's final words.

Now, moving across a wide swath of sun-dried grass,

Cleve thought about that. He had seen Pawnee and Sioux and Comanche and Cheyenne set fires to drive away enemies or to divert buffalo herds into ravines, where the great beasts lumbered forward even while their fellows were falling and being crushed beneath tons of their brethren. Food for thousands would be killed, though relatively little of it could be used and saved. It was wasteful, and his Protestant conscience knew it, but it was also a matter of survival.

A fire in this high grass would be a desperate matter, for while the flames leaped quickly through the tangle, the thickness of the grass itself impeded horse and man alike. Riding fast through it was impossible.

He didn't know the Tollivers well. They might be the sort who didn't care who they caught in the trap designed for a specific enemy. He was going to behave as if they were anyway, and that was why he kept his eyes peeled and warned Billy Wolf to speak at once if he caught any odd sound or scent.

They rode and walked and rode again for several days, stopping to rest the horses and water them from their waterskins when there was no stream handy. Creeks had become farther apart all the time they traveled. Now Cleve rose as high as he could on Socks to scan the countryside. He needed a bare place to camp. Lacking that, he'd have to clear one, for he didn't intend to be shot or knifed or roasted in his sleep.

The sun disappeared before its time into a bank of cloud. Uneasy winds rippled the grass tops, first from east and then from west, north, and south, as if some huge child blew it randomly. Cleve felt a prickle along his back.

Weather was building in the north and west, and it would be best to get Billy Wolf out of it, if possible.

There seemed no end to the sweep of grass; he rode forward, veering back toward the east, where there were more trees and creeks for shelter from a big wind. At last he saw a dark mass against the pewter sky, which was streaked with angry scarlet, for the setting sun had eased below the cloud layer and was now halved by the horizon.

They rode forward blindly after sunset, but Cleve had his direction firmly in mind, and they arrived among the first scanty growth of trees before the wind became too strong. Deeper into the wood there was a tangle that had been created by some past storm, the tree trunks crisscrossed and twisted and broken. When he kindled a torch with the coals he had brought in a clay-lined gourd from his mother's fire, replenished every night from his campfire, he could see in the whipping light that it should be easy to find a nook into which he and his son could fit.

The wind now roared through the trees and rain pounded the leaves and trickled through in streams onto the dust below. Cleve led the horses into the shelter of the tangle and loosed them. They wouldn't go far in weather like this.

Then he cast about, seeking for a spot high enough to keep them dry and low enough to protect them from the debris flung by a tornado, if one came ripping out of the night. But it was the pup, Jase, who located the perfect spot.

A shrill yip made Cleve look up to find the little dog sitting on the root ball of a downed tree. When he moved toward the pup, Jase retreated, and there behind the earth clump was a sort of tunnel. It was floored by the trunk of the fallen tree and its roof and farther sides were made of interlaced branches and trunks of those that had fallen across it. Vines had climbed over and through the entire mess.

High enough and low enough, he decided. "Come on, Billy Wolf. Let's get our hides up there. We can dry out over our torch ... can't see building any fire when the wind might scatter it to kingdom come and burn us up."

The boy came slowly, and Cleve knew he was exhausted. The long ride and the painful grooves in his arm and side had combined to quench his usual high spirits. He lifted the child and set him in the opening of this impromptu shelter.

Snip and Jase moved forward ahead of Billy Wolf, sniffing and growling, though now the wind was so strong that it was hard to hear them. Any snakes that might be there would be scared away, which was good.

Cleve dragged the heavy pack of blankets and food up with a leather rope and began spreading the buffalo robe to make a water-resistant roof over them. There were plenty of stubs to tie it to, and once it was in place, the rain hit them only occasionally when blown under the edges.

Then he heard the roar and he knew if he had chosen badly this would be the end of them. Second Son would never know what happened to her family, and his people would not realize they should mourn. A tornado, sure enough, accompanied the storm across the flat country.

Dousing the torch by thrusting it out into the downpour, he caught his son to his chest and wedged himself between the big tree trunk and an intersecting stub. The robe billowed and flapped, trying to tear away from its ties, but it held.

Blown leaves suddenly filled the small space, stinging his face, and he buried Billy Wolf in his arms and leaned his head against the boy's. There were crashes and the groans of breaking wood even over the sound of the wind as he tried to become part of the tree on which he sat.

Then the roar was less, diminishing as it passed into the distance, and he could breathe again.

Billy Wolf moved, half-stifled. When Cleve released him, the boy asked, his voice very quiet, "Was that what my mother calls a devil wind?"

Cleve rummaged for his gourd that held the carefully nurtured coals from home and thrust a bit of branch, kept dry by the robe, into the glow until flames began to curl up from the broken fibers. By that light he looked into his son's face.

Dark, shuttered, unafraid: the boy was all Tsistsistas. He hadn't learned fear from his white-skinned kindred, and that was good.

"It was, my son. Definitely it was," he said.

He whistled the signal to Socks and Blaze. After a moment a whinny answered him. That was Socks. He whistled again, making it loud and clear.

In the distance there came a wild scream. That was Blaze, and he was in trouble. But it wasn't sensible to go out into the mess the tornado left behind until he could see. The horse must wait until first light.

"He'll be all right?" Billy Wolf's eyes were wide, but his face was properly expressionless.

"He sounds scared, not hurt," Cleve reassured him. "He'll wait until morning. Then we'll fix whatever's wrong."

He just hoped it would be that easy.

Billy Wolf knew that a Tsistsistas who tried to kill another of his tribe fouled the Sacred Arrows, the protection of the People. He was considered rotten, and none of his kind would ever again share any implement or vessel with him for fear of contamination. Second Son had taught him about such matters from his infancy.

Those white men who tried to kill him were not strangers. The boy knew that; his uncle Gene had called them by name. Were they members of the Bennett tribe? Or were they outsiders, who could kill without loss of honor?

There had been no word about driving them out, so he

thought they must be outsiders or enemies. He wondered if their own band might follow to take vengeance, and when Cleve warned him to keep alert for anything unusual, he felt in his heart that more than a part of that warning had to do with the men who had shot him.

The storm came as something of a surprise. In the mountains there were blizzards that buried valleys in snow and blew wanderers off the sides of mountains. But the bellowing winds that swept over them in the night were something new.

His father's big warm presence was a comfort for more than keeping away the damp and chill. Cleve was strong enough to combat even the devil winds, Billy Wolf felt certain.

They slept at last, with both dogs cuddled on top of their feet, to the steady drip of wet off the trees. Billy Wolf woke when Cleve moved gently to disengage his arms. A twinge of agony made him set his teeth before he struggled to his knees and began rolling the blanket on which they had lain. His side and arm were so stiff and painful that it was hard to move, much less to do his accustomed chores.

Cleve's big shape was dim in the narrow cubbyhole as he loosed their "roof" and moved to the opening to drop into the mud beneath. Cleve reached up to take the roll of blankets as Billy Wolf handed them down, and then the two of them secured the bundle inside the buffalo robe and tied it to a branch.

The pups jumped down to stretch and sniff about the damp ground, leaving the boy to come at his own pace. Every motion felt like hot knives as the edges of the grooves in his flesh flexed and scabs of blood broke and crumbled. But Billy Wolf said nothing as he set off behind his father.

They raised no whistle for the horses. Socks would likely be near Blaze, and once they found the stallion, they would have both in hand. It was now the tenuous light before dawn, and other people might be moving who would not have been out in the night and the storm. Both had noted the direction from which the scream of the horse had come, and without a word they moved toward it, working their way through fresh mazes of downed green timber and newly disturbed traps of dead wood.

A bird gave a startled *chirr* and bolted into the sky. Something moved amid the tangle of old timber, but it was not a man, and they ignored it. Billy Wolf touched his father's elbow and quirked an eyebrow, pursing his lips in a pantomimed whistle.

His small hands cupped together to form the shape of a bird, and Cleve nodded decisively. Billy Wolf had listened intently to the calls of every sort of creature in this new country and taught Blaze to come at the call of a mourning dove. As a result the horse had spent quite a lot of time while in Missouri trying to track down real doves, but now he might at least whinny in reply.

The fluttering call rose into the morning, and the boy was proud of its accuracy. His mother would be interested in this slightly different dove call when he got home again.

In the distance a discouraged whicker sounded through the trees. Blaze had answered.

They turned toward the sound, moving gently through the wet brush, the sodden layers of old leaves, and the interlaced webs of branches and treetops downed by this latest tornado. Cleve stepped softly, his head up, his gaze flicking from right to left, up and down, as if he felt a presence here that might be a danger to them.

Billy Wolf came behind like a silent shadow, his bright dark eyes alert. He held himself a bit stiffly to keep from disturbing the wounds, but he did not allow his pain to make him careless.

Another dove call mourned through the trees, this one from north and east. It was a real dove this time, and the horse answered it again, as if almost exhausted. But there was a strange note in the animal's voice that made Billy Wolf prick up his ears.

Cleve stopped and reached back to touch his son's shoulder. Obediently the boy sank into a clump of brush. The two dogs lay flat beside him, his hands on their heads, and he knew neither would make a sound. He had worked hard to make sure of that.

His father bent low and moved out of sight, no wet bush or sapling moving to show where he passed. Billy Wolf knew that he intended to scout out the young stallion's location. Walking into some kind of trap was not a thing those trained by the Tsistsistas were stupid enough to do.

There were other people than those Tollivers who might follow them along the rivers and on the plains. Some were not good to meet unexpectedly ... or at all.

The sky lightened to silver and then to gold. The treetops, bedraggled and tattered by the storm, loomed like black lace against the high layers of cloud. The scanty wood filled with the morning calls of many birds and the *zooning* sounds of locusts grew louder and more continuous.

Suddenly the insect sounds stopped short and a crow cawed warningly from a nearby treetop. The boy didn't move, but he was tense and ready, his knife in his left hand since his right arm was disabled. That might be his father returning, disturbing the creatures, though Cleve would signal soon, if it were he. Or it might be something else.

A twig cracked sharply, and a jaybird went shooting out of a young oak. Billy Wolf moved silently to lie flat beside the pups and the three wriggled forward to hide beneath an edge of the tumble of downed trees.

Peering out into the growing light, he saw, through stems of weeds and damp ruffles of drifted bark, a movement that turned into a pair of feet in white man's boots. Snip almost growled, but a firm hand on his back silenced him. Jase merely went very still, though the boy could feel him vibrating with tension.

Billy Wolf felt the thud of steps in the ground, though the walker was trying to go quietly. Another pair of feet appeared on the game path, smaller than the first but still big enough to indicate a sizable man.

Where was his father? No sound came from the direction from which Blaze's whinny had sounded. There was no birdcall in Cleve's peculiarly sharp and effective style. What should he do?

He did nothing, lying as invisible as a snake in his covert while the boots went past. The vibrations stopped just beyond his position, and a gruff voice, trying to speak softly, said, "Where them bastards gone, Jim? I'da swore somebody'd have come to see about that trapped horse, but never a sign. If we could've caught the gelding, we'd've been sure of 'em. You suppose the twister got 'em?"

"Could be. If it didn't, we will, you can bank on that. Now shut your yap and let me listen, Deke."

There was a long moment of quiet, though not of silence. A katydid, encouraged by the rain of the night before, set up its kazooing in the cool of the morning, and a flight of small dark birds settled in a tree overhead and began to chatter. From the south and east came a discouraged whimper from the trapped horse.

"They might be blowed clean to Chiny," said the first voice. "That was some humdinger of a storm. Good thing we holed up or we might've took off, too."

Jim grunted. "Ought to be some sign of 'em, someplace. They was heading back this way when the cloud started coming up. That spyglass you stole from the army come in handy for keepin' track without getting in easy sight of that booger. But it can't see in the dark, and that's when we lost 'em. Let's go up this way and see what we can find."

The feet moved off in the direction of the night's camp, but there was no dead fire as indication of anyone's camping there. Then Billy Wolf thought of that betraying bundle hanging on the stub of branch. It was as plain as the marks in the book his grandmother had kept trying to teach him to read, back in Missouri.

He quavered his dove call again, muting the sound with cupped hands. From a distance there came the cry of a hawk. Cleve's hawk, sharp and easy and real sounding. His father was alive and had some scheme afoot.

When he could no longer hear the steps or the voices, the boy crawled out of his hiding place. He put Jase on the spot where Cleve had last seen them and motioned for him to stay. The pup lolled his tongue from the corner of his mouth and gazed up pleadingly, but the boy was firm. A downward motion told him to stay. He would, Billy Wolf knew.

Snip wagged his skinny tail, waiting his turn. The boy

motioned toward the trees south of the downed timber, and when he moved, the pup went with him. Once amid the trees, Billy Wolf raced back toward the spot where the supplies had been stashed, keeping his feet clear of noisy debris and his ear tuned for any sound from those he followed.

He slowed and stopped before he came too close. Here the bushes grew thickly, for the fallen trees had let sunlight into what used to be thick woods. That offered good cover, and he wriggled forward through the prickly branches, knowing that the leaves would hide him well enough from men who would be trying to decide what to make of the bundle of robes and food.

"They been here, sure enough," Deke was saying. "This here's Injun stuff, and no mistake. The mud's all tracked up, too, so they must be headed off to find that horse. Why didn't we catch sight of 'em?"

"Sneaky bastards," said Jim. "Lije told me, before we come away, that Bennett done took up with savages, away out yonder, and brung his half-Injun young'un home with him to torment his little nieces." There was the sound of hawking and spitting, as if the man hated the taste of the words.

"Who knows what heathen tricks he's learned, out yonder among the wild'uns? We better go careful, Deke. Wouldn't surprise me if he'd learned to lift hair with the best of 'em."

Billy Wolf crept forward a bit more, keeping an eye on the two as they searched the ground around the downed tree where the bundle had been left. They were no trackers, he could see at once. They were stomping out as many

tracks as they were finding, messing up the muddy ground
with their booted feet.

He kept a hand on Snip's neck, feeling the hair bristle
as the young dog watched these intruders into their camp.
Billy Wolf lay beside the pup, wondering what he should
do. He had no way of knowing what Cleve planned or
from which direction his father might appear. Then he
felt, through his elbows and belly, the impact of hooves on
soil.

Cleve had found Socks or Blaze. That was his first
thought. Socks would not have left the stallion trapped,
and Blaze would not come alone if he were free. But there
was only one set of thuds, so it was reasonable to expect
one horse.

His bow had been left with their supplies, for with his
bad arm he couldn't manage even the child's weapon. He
had nothing except his knife, and he laid that on the
ground before him, ready for use at any instant.

He hoped Snip would attack if things became dangerous, but the little dog hadn't yet learned much about battle. Even the big dogs belonging to the Bennetts hadn't
been hostile to the Indian pup. More curious than anything, in fact.

Billy Wolf sighed. He could only wait and wonder while
his father worked things out.

chapter
— 17 —

Cleve moved through the tangled growth, slipping past
downed trees and through broken vines in the soundless
manner he had been taught. The horse whinnied again,
sounding distressed, and as he neared the source of the
noise he bent and crawled beneath the layered debris, setting his hands and knees cautiously.

He heard the crushing sound of a big body straining
against wood and the sharp rap of hooves pawing at some
obstruction. That must be Blaze trying to get free of whatever windfall had him confined. But over that sound there
was another, the slap of leather against flesh.

The horse screamed and the crashing of branches became louder. Someone was tormenting the stallion, whipping him or slapping at him with something.

Cleve sped forward on his belly, knowing that any noise he made would be covered by the struggles of the young stallion. As he neared the end of the tangle he saw four legs, ending in leather boots. White men, without doubt. Indians had more sense than to torture their feet with such footgear.

He slid backward and headed through a maze of broken wood for the lighter spot on his right, well away from the men, who obviously intended to lure him into ambush when he came to rescue the horse. As he crept out of concealment he heard a soft *whuff*. He turned his head to find Socks staring at him from a thicket, where he had obviously hidden from the strangers.

Cleve rose cautiously and went to the gelding, gentling him as he put a leather line about his neck and led him away around the downed young trees. He would not dance to the tune those men piped. He would work his way back beyond the route he had taken and watch to see if the pair became impatient and began to search the wood.

He was not concerned for his son. The boy knew to keep hidden and to move only when it was safe. The intensive work they had put into training the young dogs was going to pay off well now, for instead of betraying them, the pups might be of help.

He hated to turn his back on Blaze, but once he had settled these two, he would return and free the horse. Socks knew all the tricks of walking softly and followed him quietly, his ears cocked, not even whiffling through his nostrils.

Cleve found a good spot from which to watch the scanty growth around the old heap of deadfall. A clump of brush had grown tall and thick enough to conceal him, once he mounted Socks and looked out over the gray-brown mass of lichened logs and tops. While he could see fairly clearly, anyone on the game track at the other side of the debris would be frustrated by the dusty-green leaves that hid him.

It didn't take long. And once the two emerged from the trees and into the strong morning light, he knew at once who they were. The long Tolliver bones, the narrow Tolliver faces with deep-sunk eyes and dark beards were as near as nothing the duplicates of those belonging to Lije and Carter, who had shot his son.

These two intended to take revenge for the humiliation and confinement of their kin, he understood at once. He'd already noted among the trappers and traders that those with the least to be proud of seemed to carry family pride to crazy extremes.

The Tollivers had been up on Horse Creek before the Americans ever got into that part of Missouri. Their name was so outlandish it had been shortened almost at once to something more manageable. They had never fitted in smoothly with their Scotch-Irish and German neighbors. They were troublemakers from the word go and always had been.

Cleve grimaced unconsciously, his hands gripping Socks's mane, his gaze steady on the intruders. They moved up the path, and when they came to the thicket that blocked his view, he touched Socks lightly with his heels and the horse backed out of their hiding place and headed quietly around the tumble toward the spot where he and his son had spent the night. That betraying bundle of supplies was sure to catch their attention.

He slid off Socks at a considerable distance from the fallen tree. Looping the line up so it wouldn't trip the gelding, he put his hand on the horse's forelock, whose gay dangle of scarlet feathers moved gently in the morning breeze, and looked into his eyes.

This animal had been his friend for a lot of years. He was past middle age, becoming a bit slower than he had been, but what time had taken away in speed it had added in training and basic good sense. It was almost as if he read the horse's mind and the horse read his.

With a final pat, Cleve turned silently toward the farther side of the area where he had camped the night before. He could hear the clumping steps of the men, who seemed not to know to avoid making noise as they moved. He crept around the intervening tangle and came up quietly beyond the tree in time to hear a murmured conversation between the two as they trampled about, trying to read tracks left in the mud.

He wondered if the boy remained in hiding where he had left him or if he had shadowed the steps of the men as they came this way. Whatever it was, they obviously had no idea anyone was near at hand.

"We know they didn't go all the way back there, 'cause we come through the woods, and it's too skimpy to hide anybody. Either they taken off north or south, or they're hiding someplace. Whichever it is, we better go back and get our horses."

The other hawked and spat. "If we set out there in the open, hid out in the grass, and watch with the glass, we'll see 'em when they finally make up their minds to come out and get on with their trip. Sooner or later they've got to move."

They trampled back the way they had come, seeming to take no precautions against ambush. If they got to their horses, they would be harder to deal with, Cleve knew. He needed to tackle them right now.

He gave the whistle that brought Socks into action. Before the men on the path could react, the gelding was beside him, and he vaulted onto his bare back and kneed him after their quarry.

He hadn't reached the root where they had camped when two balls of fur came shooting out of the edge of the wood south of the windfall, one yipping softly, the other, teeth bared, making silently for vulnerable legs. Behind came a wiry figure, knife in hand, urging the dogs on with shrill cries.

"It's that damn Injun brat!" the taller man shouted. "Git him, Deke!"

As the chunky Tolliver primed his rifle and aimed Cleve came around a bend in the path, bent low over Socks's neck. Deke wheeled toward the new threat, but both dogs set needle-sharp puppy teeth in his calves and he went down with a shriek. The rifle, ready to fire, sent its ball harmlessly into the treetops.

The taller of the Tollivers had been caught with his rifle unloaded, which was a basic error no sensible man would have allowed to happen. He was ramming the patch desperately with his whipstick when Cleve pounded past, leaning from Socks's back to knock the weapon from his hands. Then he was on his pursuer, rolling over the rubble of broken wood that strewed the pathway.

Busy with the struggling man beneath him, Cleve still heard a curse from the other Tolliver and increased snarling and snapping from the pups. But he had no time to attend to that, for the farmer had the oaklike strength of his kind, muscles knotted like granite from years of toil, clearing rocks from his fields, chopping wood, carrying heavy burdens.

The man had little skill at rough-and-tumble fighting, but he had determination and nerve to spare. No sooner did Cleve think he had him pinned helplessly than with a snakelike wriggle the fellow managed to turn and unseat him. They grappled, bit, scratched, and cursed, neither gaining the advantage for a long time.

"Injun lover," Tolliver gasped at last, "we'll git you yet. And we'll gut your brat! My kin'll go back and burn out your folks, too." He spat up into Cleve's face, and the world went red.

For a moment the mountain man had a vision of that wicked old buffalo he had seen long ago along the Missouri, its coat bright with frost and morning light. Those red eyes burned through the fog like those of the devil himself. That was when he thought himself damned, though he'd overcome that notion in the years afterward.

Now the evil strength of that vision surged through him, blurring his vision, burning in his veins, filling him with a fury that was not that of a devil but of a father whose child is threatened. He strained to roll again, for Tolliver had managed to get on top once more.

With a maniacal burst of strength, Cleve forced his opponent over and down. The skinny arms clawed at him, raking his face with dirty nails, trying for his eyes. The face swam into focus, teeth bared, eyes tight shut with effort, but now Cleve was riding the crest of his fury.

With a sweeping motion, he freed his arms and got his hands on Tolliver's neck. It broke like a stick in his grasp, and the body beneath him quivered and flopped like a chicken whose neck had been wrung. The tang of urine was acid in his nostrils as he rose slowly from the body and turned to deal with Deke.

That proved to be unnecessary. He was down flat on his back, a dog holding on to each hand with steely teeth, Billy Wolf sitting on his chest, holding his knife to the man's throat with his left hand.

Cleve caught his breath, his heart still thudding with effort. Then he laughed, the booming sound filling the wood.

"Looks like we two make a pair, son," he said to Billy Wolf. "But you better let me get a hold on that one. I don't want you to have to cut his throat and get yourself all dirty."

The boy rose, still bending to keep the knife in place as he stepped off the recumbent Tolliver. When Cleve pulled the pups off the man's arms—not too gently—Deke's eyes rolled in his grimy face, and he let out a yip to match the dogs'.

"You're going to stand up and face me and keep your hands and feet still. You understand me?" Cleve kept his voice calm, though he wanted to break this one's neck to match his brother's.

"Unh!" Sweat was forming in big drops on the low forehead.

"Now come up easy, because I'll kill you if you go for a knife." He backed off a couple of steps, Billy Wolf keeping pace with him, and watched intently as Deke Tolliver heaved onto his butt, then rolled to push himself up with hands that dribbled blood from the tooth marks left by the two pups.

There was a line of blood on his neck, too, where the boy's knife had sliced lightly into the skin, and it marked his filthy homespun shirt with crimson. Deke coughed hard and spat, the sound almost a sob. "You better watch your back, you Bennett bastard."

Tolliver almost choked, got his breath, and slowly swiped his sleeve across his face, where sweat was making tracks through the grime. "I got more kin than a dog has fleas," Deke said, his voice breaking.

"They're a half day behind us, a bunch of 'em, keepin' out of range till we got you treed. Now you've kilt my brother, they'll never quit. Lije and Carter won't stay cooped up longer than it takes our cousins to git 'em out, and then a whole passel more'll be after you and your bastard brat like a swarm of bees."

"They will?" asked Cleve, feeling the warmth of fury begin to build again inside him. "You sure of that?"

Deke looked puzzled. "You can kill me if you want, but they'll git you in the end, I can guarantee that. Tollivers never give up a blood feud, no matter what. If they should happen to lose you two, they'll go back and wipe out your folks, now that you've managed to kill Jim. And if you do anything nasty to me, it'll be worse. They'll finish what that Injun began with them little girls. Won't a one of your kin be alive if they don't git you."

"Thank you for explaining that to me," Cleve said. Rage kept his voice low, but his son, feeling the depths beneath the words, looked up at him, his eyes worried and wary.

"Now turn and move toward those trees behind you— yes, the pair close together." Cleve kept a couple of paces distance as he followed his captive. "Now stop and stand right there. Billy Wolf, you get the extra line out of that bundle."

The boy ran back to the pack, which the Tollivers had cut down and left lying in the mud. In a moment he returned with the coil of rope, a gift from Gene, who'd spared a length of his new hemp rope purchased from a peddler from St. Louis. The boy flipped a span free and moved from the side to tie Deke's feet together.

Cleve gestured with his knife, and Tolliver put his hands behind his back. Billy Wolf cut a handy length and bound those, too.

"Now I'll finish up," Cleve said. "You step back and keep a sharp eye on him, son, in case he tries something. Keep the pups ready to jump him, too." He almost grinned, so intent were the three young creatures on his movements.

He flipped his knife and set the blade inside the neck of the man's shirt, slicing downward to lay open his clothing from throat to crotch, from crotch to ankles. In a moment Deke was naked as a rock. Then Cleve looped Tolliver in a veritable spiderweb of rope, tying him between the trees so it was impossible for him to move.

"Make a gag," he said to Billy Wolf, and the boy caught up a thick end of broken branch, one-handed, and broke it short. Laboriously he tied thongs to secure it behind the man's head. Cleve forced Tolliver's jaws apart so they had to clamp down on the wood.

"So here you stay and wait for all those kinfolk to come and rescue you," he told the squirming captive. "It'll get a bit chilly maybe, and you won't be comfortable, but unless you're a weakling, that won't bother you much.

"Now we're going to get our horses and our supplies and haul our tails out of here. Say hello to the Tolliver clan for us and tell 'em we'll be waiting for 'em someplace in the grasslands. Maybe with reinforcements." That was bravado, Cleve knew, but it made Tolliver wince.

Billy Wolf swayed on his feet, and Cleve scooped the child into his arms and headed for the pack. "You stay here and watch our stuff. I'll go and cut Blaze loose from the trees that fell around him. Then we'll be on our way, all right?"

Billy Wolf nodded and settled against the fallen tree, sitting on the pack with a pup on either side of him. As Cleve whistled Socks up again and headed for the trapped stallion, he wondered if he would manage to get them both out of this mess alive. He had heard tales of Tollivers when he was smaller than his son. They were mean and ignorant and as persistent as mosquitoes.

That was a bad combination. He was going to have to travel fast and keep a sharp eye on his back trail to have any chance of outrunning them. And once he'd done that, he was going to have to circle wide and get between them and the rest of the Bennetts. He wasn't about to have his people slaughtered by a bunch of filthy Tollivers.

chapter

— 18 —

They wasted no time. Once Cleve freed the stallion, he lifted Billy Wolf onto Blaze's back, loaded the pack of supplies, and they set off to the northwest at a quick walk.

There was no use in tiring the horses until it was necessary, so they fell into a steady pace, moving through the dried grasses of late summer, the tall seed heads switching at their knees and rustling beneath the horses' hooves. Above them the tall clouds sailed on the constant wind, and occasional birds rose on whirring wings before their animals' hooves.

When they dismounted to stretch their legs and rest

their mounts, Cleve turned and tried to look behind them. But the buffalo grass was too tall and thick, even dried as it was. When he remounted, standing easily on Socks's back, he wasn't able to see far enough to make out anything in the distance.

He was sure he knew when Deke had lied and when he told the truth. With Tollivers, that wasn't too hard to do. The "bunch" of Tollivers their kinsman claimed to be after them was probably right there, but he doubted their numbers. That family fought too fiercely among themselves to get together more than a couple of dozen able to cooperate on any important common project. So he banked on having maybe four or five of the long-headed bastards on his trail for this minor skirmish.

It might be they hadn't found Deke yet. That would depend on how far behind their scouts they were and what sort of trackers they might be when they found their kinsman's body and looked around for his brother. Judging by the two he had watched, Cleve thought his chances of having anyone on his tail before dark were pretty slim.

He had found and confiscated the spyglass when he located it while slicing off Deke's clothing. Even that revealed no pursuit, and when the sky began to darken in the east while he made his last scan, Cleve put the thing away. It was time to find water for the horses and shelter from the wind for Billy Wolf. A wound led to fever, and he didn't want to have to deal with a serious sickness on such a precarious journey.

The boy had been feverish, of course, off and on through the day. Ma had sent some of her herbal mix for him to boil up at night in order to keep the fever down. She'd sent a pot of ointment, too. Cleve dropped behind his son, watching the small body sag on Blaze's back and streaks of blood seep out to widen on the dirty bandages about his arm and chest.

It was time to stop, if he could find a fairly well concealed place to camp. The long shadows crept across the grassland, making it hard to distinguish the long streak that might denote a creek's fringe of willows or cottonwoods.

Cleve kept straining his eyes, seeking something less obvious, something that anyone tracking them might well not consider an appropriate place for a man to camp with a wounded child.

He saw trees far to the north, but he ignored them. That would be the first place anyone would look. The boy began to waver on the stallion's back, and he rode up beside him and caught his son into his arms, setting him before him on Socks's steady back.

Then the gelding snorted and raised his head, ears pricked forward. Socks turned from their route and headed off at an angle, picking up speed.

Cleve relaxed. His old friend smelled water. After so many years in the mountains and the plains, he had learned to trust the animal's senses and his instincts. If Socks said that was the way to go, he was ready to accept it.

Night swept the last light from the west, and stars began to blaze from the endless sky. Without knowing where they were going, Cleve gave the gelding his head and let him find his own way, and the animal never faltered.

Then Blaze whickered, sensing at last the water the older horse had recognized before the scent was strong. The pair of them began to trot, then to gallop, and Cleve's arms cushioned Billy Wolf against the motion. When Socks slowed and stopped, he sat for a moment, trying to see or hear anything that might be nearby.

He heard the trickle of water, even above the constant bluster of the wind. Random gusts whistled through crevices, and he knew that his mount had brought him to some rocky formation near a stream.

Cleve swung his legs over and dropped to the ground, still holding his son carefully. Billy Wolf grunted softly as they landed, but he didn't whimper.

"When I was your age, I'd have cried like a baby," Cleve murmured to the boy. "You're Tsistsistas, son, and nobody can say better than that."

"I can stand up," came the quiet reply, and he set the child on his feet.

Cleve fumbled for his fire gourd, into which he had fed chips from the deadfall where they spent the previous night. Red still glowed when he shook the gourd; he felt about and gathered a bunch of dried grass, which he twisted into a skimpy torch and thrust into the coals. In the blaze of red-gold light, he crouched and looked around.

The horses stood together inside an arc of rocks higher than his head; they were weathered into curves on top but split into layers on the sides. Where the stream had cut through stone, a pool glittered, and the sound Cleve had heard came from a thin fall of water that trickled from a shelf some yard higher.

A willow had grown from a crack between two of the rock layers and died, and Cleve wrenched off several of the dry branches and laid them neatly in a sheltered niche among the rocks, where the light of a fire would be invisible from the plain. He laid out the sleeping robes and put Billy Wolf beside the blaze.

Mama had insisted that he take one of her precious iron pots, small enough to pack but large enough to contain sufficient stew or broth for a couple of people. He dug it out. Arranging stones beside the blaze, which was now being fed with large chunks of dead willow, he boiled water for the herb tea that helped to control fever. He added strips of willow bark to help combat the fever, though it would make the stuff even more bitter.

After dosing the boy with the hot tea and feeding him, Cleve unwrapped the old bandages and put them into the fire. Soft rags, saved carefully by his mother for use as bandages, also had been put into his supply roll, and now he cleaned the wounds, smeared ointment liberally onto the angry flesh, and re-bound his son's injuries.

He buried the fire in ash and dust, but poured no water onto the hot coals. The acrid steam had a unique scent, and anyone who knew what he was doing would detect it even over a distance.

Billy Wolf was drowsing, his belly full, his pain eased. Cleve lifted him again and took him, along with the bedroll, beyond the rough arc of stones and up the dry wash running down to the stream to a hidden nook amid a clump of cottonwoods.

There he bedded the boy down and left him in the care of the two dogs while he went after the horses. You didn't sleep where you had your fire, and you didn't sleep beside water. He knew greenhorns who had died because they didn't know that.

Cleve had no intention of sleeping. With Tollivers out there looking for him, it would have been stupid even to doze. He crawled up into the layered rocks, which were still warm from the day, but he wrapped a buffalo robe around him, for the wind was chilly once the sun was gone.

There was no moon, but the sky was bright with stars, and no cloud moved to dim their glare. He could see a bit from that height, for the dry tan grasses were pale in the starlight. Any horse or man moving close by would show up as a dark blot against that paleness. He could look down into the cottonwoods that hid his son. He could see the horses grazing in the ravine.

It was a good lookout, and situated as he was between two thick thumbs of weathered stone, he couldn't be spotted against the sky by anyone scouting out the area. Cleve sat cross-legged, his back straight, his head up. He might doze later, but for now he was wide-awake.

Any Tolliver coming out of the night was going to get a terrible surprise, although, knowing the family from old gossip, he felt they would never take the trouble to track their quarry in darkness. *Slack-twisted* was the way his mother had always referred to them, when they came to her disdainful attention.

The stars turned westward, wheeling across the night and moving down beyond the distant horizon. He regularly swept the dim plain with his searching gaze and even used the glass, but nothing moved. Only coyotes howled and night birds called.

At last Cleve's eyelids grew heavy and he leaned against one of the stumps of stone, resting his back, relaxing his body without relaxing his attention. Second Son had taught him many handy tricks her people used to control their bodies, and this was one of the most valuable.

He closed his eyes frequently, resting them without allowing himself to drift into sleep. Opening them after one such rest, Cleve realized that there was a glow to the south. Though there were no clouds to reflect it, he knew that a grass fire was burning there, and he wondered if his pursuers were carrying through Deke's threat to trap and destroy him as the inferno raged through the tinder-dry grass.

Though the blaze had to be miles away, its light just now visible on the horizon, Cleve knew too well how swiftly the dried grasses burned. He had been on raids with his Tsistsistas brother-in-law, helping fire the grass behind a fleeing herd of stolen horses to keep their owners from taking a direct route in pursuit. It was also a nasty but effective strategy if you wanted to kill someone you knew to be traveling through the high growth but couldn't quite locate.

The Tollivers were just low enough to try that method of destroying someone who was too fast and too tough for them to tackle hand to hand. Even while he thought what the distant glow might mean, Cleve was dropping off his rocky perch and scrambling up the ravine toward his sleeping son.

Snip growled softly, and he calmed the pup and hissed through his teeth to reassure Jase. Billy Wolf was deeply asleep, and he folded the bedrobe about his small body and carried him to the rocks, where he put him safely on a flat space, well clear of the edge and above anything that might burn.

He pitched the two pups up with the boy, once he was down again. They peered at him anxiously over the edge as he moved to collect the horses and lead them into the bare space within the arms of the stone. By the time he had them tethered to the remnant of the willow stump, the sky was alight from side to side and the leaping gold of flames was already visible.

The fire was moving against the breeze, its increasing heat igniting the thick grass and creating its own focus to draw wind into the updraft. Cleve had seen many grass fires while he lived with the Tsistsistas, and Singing Wolf had explained to him what happened when the plains burned.

This was not going to be something he could outrun, for he knew that no river was near enough for him to cross before the blaze arrived. Indeed, at this time of year any river he found might well be dry or so low that the fire would leap it without hesitation.

The wide expanse of layered stone would keep the flames away from their bodies, and the horses should be safe in the nook beside the water, where grazing buffalo had eaten any grass down to the dirt. But he knew that a suffocating cloud of gases would whirl over them as the fire passed. That was going to be dangerous.

He climbed onto the wide span of stone again and shook the drowsy boy awake. "Billy Wolf, you sit by the pups while I wet the buffalo robe. We're going to have to lie low while that burns across us." He gestured toward the red-gold line, now hurtling toward them faster than a horse could gallop.

Billy Wolf grunted with comprehension and rolled aside to sit, wide-eyed, staring at the approaching flames. Cleve left him there and went down to the pool, where he soaked the buffalo robe and swept it across the two horses' backs, wetting their manes in the process. Then he wet it again and went up the rocks, more heavily now, for he was burdened with the weight of the soaking robe.

Once the boy and the dogs were under the tough hide, he returned to the camp in the ravine and brought the bundled remains of their equipment. He wet the deerhides in which the supplies were wrapped and put the soggy mess into a wind-worn cup in the top of the rock. Then he crawled beneath the robe with his son, holding the boy in the crook of one arm and the shivering pups in the other.

The air beneath the dripping hide grew warm and then warmer. The stink of burned grass and small animals roasting and billows of smoke began to move beneath the buffalo robe. Something thudded past on frantic hooves, and he knew a buffalo or deer was fleeing for its life. Billy Wolf coughed, and Cleve felt his own eyes beginning to water, his nose clogging.

The approaching roar of the flames grew louder, and even beneath the wet hide they were hot. The drips stopped, and he could feel their covering drying as the heat intensified. The closeness of the animals and the child began to make the air beneath the robe even hotter. The stink of singeing hair was stifling there beneath their shelter.

Socks whinnied, his cry high and shrill with terror. Blaze screamed, and the crackling roar became deafening. Something cracked like a shot, and Cleve thought it might be stone snapping in the heat.

Suddenly there was no air, and he found his lungs straining to inhale, but there was nothing to breathe. He could feel the pups' sides heaving against him, and his son tensed, frightened at last by this feeling of suffocation.

There was nothing to do. Cleve held tightly to the

young creatures in his care, hearing nothing, feeling as if his skin must melt as the robe and the rock beneath him grew hot and the fire, intense and all-devouring, rushed over them. He had felt helpless in the past, many times, but never so much as he did now.

If they survived this, he'd be persuaded that he was a tough man to kill.

chapter

— 19 —

They had been riding for many days since the tornado passed over, and Second Son was beginning to wonder if she would ever come to the Missouri country Yellow Hair had talked about. On these endless grasslands, it was possible to pass the one you searched for without ever being aware that he might be within a day's ride.

But she had her vision still inside her mind: the fire and the ashy shapes rising from the burned grass pulled her forward, south and east, south and east. There was no doubt that the ones she intended to find were still ahead of her, for another dream or her sure instinct would have told her if they were not.

She knew that she would ride into the forested country and up to the very lodge of Yellow Hair's people, if she did not meet him before. He had drawn her a map in the dust of the plain, and she knew the streams and the hills that marked the location of his old home. She would find the Bennetts if she did not find her man first.

Rakes the Sky with Lightning was not so confident, she knew, though her nephew said nothing. She could tell what he was thinking by the way he glanced aside at her and then ahead, his gaze sweeping the rolling expanses before them.

They crossed swells of grass and dry flats beside creeks whose waters had diminished to damp streaks. The sky was intensely blue now, and the sun beat down mercilessly on the cracking mud as they descended into the shelter of one such stream's banks, keeping to the cottonwood-and-willow shade as long as they could. This turned out to be longer than Second Son had expected, for the serpentine course tended mainly toward her own goal.

By late afternoon they had come to a deep bend, and she urged her mount up a game-cut track and onto the plain again. It was about here that she should turn more to the south, and the stream was meandering due east.

As evening neared she and Lightning killed a rabbit and a grouse and stopped to rest and eat. Traveling at night was easier than by day, for both horses and men. Water might well be scarce as they left this last stream, for at this time of year sometimes it was days before you found a creek or water hole with enough moisture left to water horses.

A tiny fire, kindled with buffalo chips at the bottom of a wallow, scorched the meat, and they ate crouching on their heels, the horses grazing at some distance. When the fire was covered, they caught their mounts again and moved forward, still south and east, and night came down upon them.

There was little for riders on a moonless night to fear, for few rode in darkness, and only if they met someone face-to-face would they be detected. Second Son was half dozing, lulled by the slow and steady thump of her mare's hooves amid the grass and dust. Lightning, ahead of her, was slumped, too, resting while he rode.

But no Tsistsistas ever rested for long when he was not at peace in the heart of his own village. Second Son roused frequently to full alertness and checked her direction by the stars, correcting her course by sighting on the Little Bear. When her gaze moved around to survey the horizon, black against the stars, she halted at once and said, "Na'!"

Lightning straightened, and her arm went up. In the south was a pinkish glow that brightened even as they watched.

She nodded. There was the fire of which she had dreamed. Her people were there. Something inside her assured her of this, even as she turned her mount's head toward the growing blaze.

"It moves quickly, Nihu'," Lightning said. "No horse can outrun a blaze in summer grass."

She knew that, of course, and it was only instinct that had drawn her in that direction. If she was to help her family, she must survive, so she turned back on their tracks. They had crossed a wide stretch of stone and sand some hours before. Wide enough, she hoped, to save them from the fire.

Her nephew knew at once what she intended to do, and together they raced back toward that flimsy haven. Behind them the horizon turned red gold from side to side, and the acrid tang of smoke was detectable, even against the wind.

The horses, spurred by their own danger, needed no urging. Together the two galloped away from the blaze, and before the stars had moved a hand span across the sky, Second Son heard the change of surface under their hooves. Instead of the crunch of hard soil beneath dried grass, her mare's steps were dulled in sand.

She rode forward, able now to see the pale expanse of grit and pebbles marking the area for which she headed. When the surrounding grasses were lost in darkness, she paused and dropped to the ground.

Now the starlight was joined by the glow from the distant fire. It was possible to see Lightning's feathers move in his braided hair as he stared toward the burning grass at the edge of the sky. His eyes were narrow in the faint light.

"This is what you saw, Nihu'," he said. "Now I understand why you came so far without meeting the one you hoped to see. Your vision was a true one."

"I still hope to see him, in spirit if not in flesh. He will come to me before he goes to the Other Place," she replied. "And our son will come, too, when the time is right."

She sat on the ground beside her horse. The mare, her dark eyes glinting with scarlet as she watched the fire, stood firm, without moving toward the grass beyond the stretch of sand. Lightning sat on the other side, his own sorrel gelding held by the single rawhide rein.

As the fire drew nearer, snapping and growling in the grass, the sky reddened, and the stars disappeared in a pall of bloodshot smoke. The air grew warmer; a backwash of smoke stung Second Son's eyes, and she knew it was time to cover herself and young Shadow to keep sparks from singeing their hair and hide.

She stood and pulled her wide buffalo robe from her pack. "Be quiet, Little One," she said to the mare as she arranged the robe to cover most of the horse's back and head. She ducked under it herself, standing almost beneath the nervous animal.

Roars and crackles, thin screams of trapped ferrets and badgers and prairie dogs, and the whickers of the frightened horses mingled with the increased flow of wind into the vortex created by the great updraft from the flames. Second Son clung to Shadow, soothing herself as much as she did the mare, as the terrible stampede of fire burst into the nearest grasses and encircled the sandy patch in an inferno that took away her breath.

Something scorched and furry blundered blindly into her ankles, and she glanced down to see a burning rabbit leap in crazy bounds until it disappeared beyond the edge of her robe.

Shadow was quivering, her delicate legs trembling, her noisy breaths audible even above the sound of burning. Second Son smoothed the mare's neck, murmured inaudible words into her ear. Suddenly straining, she tried to hold the animal steady when she shrieked and danced sideways as some unseen ember seared her exposed haunches.

The noise passed quickly, but a pall of heat and ash swirled around their sandy protection for a long time. Both horses danced about, trying to dislodge burning bits of grass and wood that had fallen onto their hides. When the air thinned and only the glow from beyond the barren patch lit the area, Second Son rolled back the robe, which stank of burned hair, and checked Shadow's back for scorched spots.

Her own ankles were spotted with burns from the fleeing rabbit. Random patches of scorch burned steadily, though the embers that caused them were long quenched. Once Shadow was settled, she smeared tallow on her own burns.

Lightning was busy with his sorrel, and by the time both were finished a hint of cooler air diluted the ashy breath of the fire. Blots of red dotted the sweep of prairie to the south, where thicker growths of bushes or stunted trees had grown.

By that uncertain light, it was possible to move on. Second Son went forward, leading her mare and checking the footing before she risked allowing either of them onto the hot surface.

Before they had traveled long, her feet were blistered and the soles of her moccasins were scorched and stiff. She sneezed, her eyes streaming from the blown ash, and behind her Lightning coughed deeply.

This was no journey fit for warriors, but here her direction lay. Somewhere beyond this burned desolation her son waited, she felt certain, and nothing could stop her as she moved toward him.

The sky was still thick with smoke, the stars hidden. When they reached a stretch in which the last flickers of coal had died away, they were left in a darkness that seemed more profound because it followed that bright conflagration.

There was one compensation. The going was cooler, the smoke swept away after the racing flames, and both horses and warriors found it easier to travel. Drawn by the instinct that seemed stretched tight as a line between her heart and her family, Second Son began to hurry, ignoring the danger of crossing unknown turf after such a blaze.

By the time the east had lightened to gray, her eyes were so well adjusted to the gloom that the faint illumination made it possible to see. Against the edge of the sky she saw a low silhouette—one of the outcrops of layered sandstone edging ravines that streaked this part of the plain. Something inside her tensed. There! There was a place in which travelers might survive such a fire.

She stopped and waited for her nephew to come even with her. "Do you smell water?" she asked him.

"I smell ash and burned beasts," he said, his tone very weary. "Water? Wait and let me try."

He raised his head, his aquiline profile sharp against the rapidly paling sky. Drawing a deep breath, he held it for a moment. Then he turned, his features lost in the insufficient light but his voice cheerful.

"I do smell water. Not a lot. There!"

Without another word, the pair vaulted onto their weary animals and headed for the outcrop, which now, as dawn progressed, showed its pale shape more clearly against the dark ruin of the burned grass. Then the horses, who had seemed too tired and fearful to react to anything, raised their heads and whinnied loudly.

From the spot toward which they were headed there

came an answering whinny, and Second Son recognized it. That was Socks. If nothing else, one horse survived there.

She kicked Shadow sharply. The mare stretched out into a gallop, her hoofbeats sounding strange as they crackled and crunched in the brittle remnants of the grass. Ahead of them, a volley of snorts and whinnies and hoofbeats broke the dead quiet.

In a cloud of kicked-up ash, Socks and Blaze appeared, and just as the sun's rim moved above the horizon the two groups met. Though her people did not often make pets of horses, Second Son felt almost as glad to see Yellow Hair's gelding as she would to see her mate.

She whistled the signal for him to follow. Again she and Lightning sped toward the refuge where they hoped their lost ones waited. Off to the left the sun rose, reddened by the remnant of smoke in the air, to light the blackened plain. She wondered as she rode, the wind whipping the smoky braids of her hair and her scorched feathers about her neck, if she would find those ashen ghosts at the end of her ride.

Or would she find a living man and their living son? She kicked Shadow harder, and the mare fairly flew across the plain.

chapter

— 20 —

Once the fire passed, Cleve lay for a while beneath the buffalo robe, hot, breathless, but weak with relief. He could hear the pained squeaks of the horses beyond the arm of sandstone, and that reassured him. If the horses lived, slightly burned or not, they could go forward toward their goal. If they had not survived, then a terrible journey afoot over burned terrain would have faced him and his son.

At last, Snip wriggled loose and crept from beneath their shelter, which was now stiff and dry from the heat of the blaze. Jase slipped out with him, leaving Cleve to sit up and stretch his numbed arms.

When he rolled the robe back, it cracked and split. It might be good for resoling moccasins, but he could no longer use it to wrap the packs, and he was thankful that he had brought a roll of supple deerhide, which was protected inside the larger rolls on top of the rock.

Billy Wolf tried to sit and gasped with pain; evidently his wounds had stiffened while he lay still. After checking the packs, which had survived, somewhat charred, Cleve lifted the boy down on the side of the rock nearest the pool. Smoke was trapped in the rocky curve and they both coughed, eyes watering, as they moved toward the pool.

Both horses greeted them with joy when Cleve carried his son to the water and set him on a flat rock. The bandages were stiff with ointment and blood, and it took some time to soak them free and to reanoint the grooves in the child's smooth, coppery skin.

"I won't build a fire," he said to his son, once he had straightened and stared away to the south where nothing but blackened stubble and soil stretched to the edge of the sky. "We've had too much damn fire, it seems to me."

Billy Wolf grinned, and Cleve's heart lifted. He had been worried that the boy might lose, in this tense situation, the cheerful nature he had always shown. The Indian in him made him solemn beyond his years, and he was very serious about matters of importance, but the child now peeped through again.

Cleve grinned back. "We've got jerky. Water. Who needs more?" he asked.

The horses looked about for their own breakfast, but there was nothing left except the bitter leaves of the living willows, which now were withered from the heat. The animals stamped and blew while their riders ate their sparse meal and the sun touched the early-morning clouds. Then Socks raised his head and whinnied.

It was a shocking thing, for the animal had been carefully taught not to betray them to enemies. but in a heartbeat Cleve knew that if his gelding shrilled such a greeting, it was to a horse he knew. That could only mean that some friend or acquaintance was out there on the plain.

Even as he thought that, the two horses jerked loose the scorched loops holding them to the dead willow and went galloping away around the curve of rock, heading north and west. Distant replies sang through the air. Someone was coming, and Cleve prepared for battle, even though he trusted his horse.

He tucked Billy Wolf, who was still chewing his strip of jerky, into a notch of stone that curved into the rock above the cup that caught the tiny waterfall. There he was hidden from anyone peering into the sheltered area.

Cleve climbed onto the top of the formation again, lying flat, though it was still too dim for anyone to see him from any distance. He had the spyglass hanging from a thong around his neck, and he pulled it out and extended it, peering toward the north. But the image was blurred in the early light, and no amount of fiddling with the thing would bring the distance into focus.

Motion caught his eye, and he squinted through the kicked-up ash and dust left by Socks and Blaze. The wind swept it aside in a moment and he could see two riders, still small but approaching rapidly.

He took his Hawken from the soft leather sleeve in which it lay most of the time, rolled into his pack. For distance, it outdid a bow, though for close, fast work the reloading took too long.

He checked flints and frizzen, poured a measured batch of powder from the horn into the space between barrel and whipstick, and slapped the barrel sharply to settle the grains. Then he rammed home the ball and patch. Priming the pan, he laid the weapon handily beside him and watched to find who was coming through the brightening dawn.

The riders urged their horses to greater efforts, and before long Cleve rose to his feet, his gladness overcoming caution. That was Second Son on Shadow's daughter! And the young man with her was none other than Cub, the one who when a boy had taught him to use the weapons of his people.

Cleve leaped down into the curve of rock and yelled, "It's your mother! And your Nihu' Lightning! Climb out here, Son, and we'll go to meet them!"

Billy Wolf, resheathing his knife, moved surely around the edge of the pool and leaped down beside his father. He didn't grunt when he landed, though Cleve knew the jar must have pained his wounds. His small face blazed with excitement as he looked up.

He turned and darted between the rough pillars of sandstone guarding the nook that had sheltered their horses. Before his father could catch up, the boy was racing over the burned stubble, holding his arm close to his right side but making very good time.

Cleave sighed. No matter how you raised a child, he was still a wild young animal when the mood struck him. He set off wearily at a jog, keeping the boy in sight and glancing up from time to time toward the cloud of dusty ash that marked the position of the horses.

Then his son yelled shrilly, and a voice answered. Second Son. Cleve smiled and picked up his own pace.

They met among the black remnants of grass left by the fire, first the horses, who turned and galloped alongside their herd mates. Cleve and his son halted while the oncoming riders pulled up and sprang from their mounts. Though all kept properly sober expressions, Cleve could see the warm gleam of his wife's black eyes, the almost crinkle at the corners of her mouth that showed she was suppressing a smile.

Billy Wolf, still panting from his exertions, stopped beside his mother and looked up at her. "It is good to know you are well," he said, with all the solemnity of some ancient chief. Then he put his arms about her hips and buried his dark head against her side.

Rakes the Sky with Lightning took Cleve's hand in a strong grip, and though he said nothing, his bright gaze was filled with gladness. "I'm glad to see you too, Cub," Cleve told the younger man. "The more help we have, the better it's going to be."

Second Son turned sharply. "Help? Is there need, then?"

"Come back while we get our possibles," he told her. "The nasties that set the fire won't be content to stop with that. They'll go after my folks. The Tollivers don't cotton to risking their necks out here in the plains country. Too many people here that're tougher and meaner than they are."

She nodded, turned, and mounted Shadow. Reaching down, she drew her son up before her, where he sat securely in the curve of her arms. Cleve climbed onto Socks, and Lightning sprang onto his sorrel. Blaze came after them as they turned the animals' heads toward the clump of rock that was now shining golden in the sunlight.

The bundle of supplies and equipment was slightly charred, the outer layer of deerhide crumbling as Cleve took out the rest of their things and rewrapped them in a skin from the smaller roll. His Hawken he unloaded again, saving both powder and ball, and secured it in the pack.

As he worked he talked, and by the time they were ready to move again, everyone understood the possibility of a raid the Tollivers might make against his family in Missouri. Billy Wolf, in particular, was distressed and furious.

"You mean those men that shot me may hurt my cousins and uncles and grandparents?" he asked. "Just because they think we may not have died in the fire?"

"They're *low*," Cleve said, lifting the boy onto Blaze. "Mean as polecats and sneaky, too. I won't feel easy until I get back and make sure they haven't gone after the folks."

He turned to Second Son, who was already astride Shadow. "I know you want to get back west and make ready for the winter, but I really got to see about my kin," he said.

She reached to lay her strong brown hand on his shoulder. "You have fought for my people," she said. "I will protect yours. It is only just."

She wheeled the mare and set out at a brisk trot toward the southeast. Cleve, who had determined the shortest route while he waited out the fire, heeled Socks into a gallop and took the lead. "I know a way to get us back there at least as soon as those slack-twisted bastards make it," he said.

She nodded, and they fell into line, moving in ashy clouds across the burned terrain toward the Missouri country. The sun was now high, with tall clouds banked in the south, drifting lazily from west to east. By the time it was overhead, they had moved out of the burned grasses and into the golden-tan reaches bordering the scrub oaks that marked the edge of the forest country.

Having no spare horses, Cleve was forced to walk the mounts from time to time, watering them whenever they found a deep hole in an otherwise dry creek. Every time they stopped, he envisioned the descent of the Tolliver family upon the farm, his brothers surprised and perhaps killed, his mother, sister-in-law, and nieces perhaps raped and certainly molested and burned out of their homes.

He held himself down to a reasonable pace, though with some difficulty. The slow miles passed, and the sun went down before he called a halt in a scrub-oak thicket. It was a dry camp, but they had filled waterskins at the last water hole; the horses were able to drink enough to quench the worst of their thirst. He and the other adults sipped sparingly, for Billy Wolf was feverish, his small body needing all the water they could give him, boiled into one of the medicinal teas his grandmother had sent.

That night Cleve shared the watch with two others, which was a relief. Until his turn came, he slept curled about Second Son's compact shape. When he woke to Lightning's light touch at his shoulder, his first thought was for his son.

But the boy slept deeply, his forehead slightly damp; the fever had broken in the night. Between the Bennett herbal medicine and the Tsistsistas variety, he had conquered the worst of the problems brought about by his wound.

Cleve rose silently and melted into the scrubby growth that marked this easternmost edge of the grasslands. The moon was rising in the east, making dappled shadows beneath the crooked oaks. An enemy might stand a few paces distant and never know he was there. But no enemy came, though he prowled a circle around the camp, which was far from the spot where they had built their cookfire.

The horses stood dozing or grazed leisurely, disliking the tough dry grass. The two pups, possible sources of noise that might betray the travelers, were secured near Billy Wolf, and as long as they could snuggle against their young master, they were content to remain there quietly.

Again Cleve circled the camp and its sleeping tenants. Something troubled him, made him climb into one of the thicker-trunked trees to gaze as far as possible to the east.

He knew that he must rouse his companions and ride now. The horses had rested and his son was better. They must go fast, his instinct told him, if they were to reach the Little Sac in time.

He crept back into the sheltered cup where his people slept and touched Lightning, then Second Son, to rouse them. They rose instantly, alert and ready for whatever might happen, but he shook his head.

"There is no enemy here, but I feel that we must go quickly. If we are to arrive in time, we have to get our tails on the way. Something's in the wind. If those bastards that set the fire went straight back toward my people's farms, they'll be getting mighty close by now."

"Then we will go." Second Son rolled the robes with precise movements and whistled for the dogs.

Lightning came with the horses, and in a moment Cleve was astride Socks, Second Son just behind, holding Billy

Wolf, who was still asleep. Their nephew came behind with Blaze, who was on a long tether.

The pups, excited by this movement in the night, bounced about, but once they started eastward again, the two were hard put to keep up with the pace Cleve set.

As for Cleve Bennett, he rode without speaking, his gaze set on the dim reaches of scrub and grass as if he were trying to see past the night and the distance in order to learn what was happening with his people.

chapter

— 21 —

When the Tsistsistas were determined to travel quickly, the distance they could cover in a day was astonishing. The horses were stumbling with exhaustion by the time Cleve drew Socks to a halt beside a narrow trickle of water issuing from a split rock. It was already dark, but a new moon lit the east with a faint glow.

The others tumbled off their mounts, ready to stretch and to drink before the horses muddied the small basin of water that collected beneath the little fall. They had managed to reach the edge of the forested lands that fringed outward from the Missouri country, and this ledge was an outcrop from the first of the big hills, which grew taller as one traveled eastward. From here onward, water would be less of a problem, even in late summer.

Cleve worked absently, helping Second Son tend their son's healing wound. When they had built a fire in the shelter of the farther reaches of the ledge, he ate sparingly of their supply of journeycake, sent by his mother. When Billy Wolf was fast asleep against his mother's knee, Cleve looked across the fire at Second Son and Lightning.

"I have been thinking about the Tollivers. They're a slack-twisted crew, and only their grandfather Rance keeps them in line at all. My brother tells me they're all afraid of the old man. If he knew they'd shot a child, he'd pitch a fit, because Tim says he's not a bad fellow, just too old to keep a tight rein on his sons and grandsons and nephews and such. I remember him when I was a boy and Pa used to go buy seed corn from him. He wasn't so bad."

Second Son laid a light hand on her son's sleek head, and the boy moved in his sleep, muttering something unintelligible. "This grandfather . . . do you think he might control what will happen with your people?" she asked. As usual, her mind worked in tandem with his own.

Cleve nodded. "If we could get him down there to the farm, he'd likely stop the others pretty quick. Like I said, Tim swears they're poison-scared of him. But he wouldn't come with you or Lightning or with a child. He knows me—or he'd remember me, I think, from when I used to go up there with Pa.

"If I go upcreek to the Tolliver settlement, it'll take me another day to get there and back, and that's if the old man doesn't take a lot of persuading. But the rest of that bunch is going to get to Pa's place before us, even the way we're traveling. Can you go and see what you can do to help while I run up the country and get old Rance?"

"Our son knows the way; he will lead us when we get to the river you described to me," Second Son replied. "We will ride fast and get there as quickly as possible. If there can be talk instead of blood, it is a good thing. Now we will sleep."

She pushed ash over the small heap of fire, and darkness settled over the camp. Cleve sat with his back against the gently sweating rock, listening to the night: the sound of the horses nipping grass under the nearby trees, the chirp of a night bird overhead, the soft swish as an owl passed over.

In the distance there was a rumble, and he knew that a bunch of buffalo must be moving along the edge of the grassland, perhaps disturbed by some predator. To the east a howl told him of a hunting wolf. But no sound of man or horse disturbed him before Second Son awoke and came to take the watch.

They were moving before dawn, the dust-dry summer air as yet cool, the horses rested and ready to travel. Cleve knew this part of the country, for he had come as a child with a party hunting for meat, one year when cattle and hogs died down to barely enough for breeding stock because of some strange disease.

Even the deer and the buffalo had been scarce that year. The hunters had combed this country, and he found that the terrain was stuck in his mind, every creek and hill of it. That was convenient now, for it allowed him to make a beeline toward the point at which he must branch off from the route the others must take.

Before night they came to the junction of two creeks

that he had chosen for splitting his party. They did not stop to camp, for now they were within a hard day's travel of the farm on the Little Sac.

Second Son turned young Shadow after Blaze and a suitably proud Billy Wolf. Lightning, on his sorrel, moved to lift a laconic hand to Cleve. Then they took their separate routes, and Cleve heeled Socks into a trot toward Horse Creek.

There the Tolliver clan raised children and corn for whiskey with equal success. There old Rance Tolliver would be sitting on his porch, feet up, head back, dozing amid the clamor of his huge brood.

The horse was tired now, and he didn't trot for long. As the sun went down, Cleve dismounted and walked, leading his gelding, watching for the tricky trail that his brother had reminded him about. There was a short way to get to Horse Creek, and this was it.

The spring, when he found it, was hidden amid thick ferns, and on each side was a bastion of gray rock. Now he was in deep forest, and it was cool, even so late in the year, as he peered into the dim recesses, finding at last a deer track, then another. He followed those to the water, and there, sidling along the narrow channel, was a path beneath the ferns.

He moved up the slot of stone, where night had already set its seal, but at the farther end there was a patch of sky and a last ray of sun lightening the top of an oak to gold. He could travel a bit farther before darkness fell.

Night found him in a dell of oak trees, and he took the opportunity to rest Socks and to sleep for a time. But in a few hours he was moving again, still toward the creek where the Tolliver clan farmed and hunted and quarreled among themselves. By the time the sun was above the tree-tops, he had reached Horse Creek, far below the Tolliver land, and was heading upstream.

The first of the solid log cabins came into view at mid-afternoon. Settled into its scraped patch of yard and sur-rounded by a thick ring of trees and bushes, it looked like some mossy animal crouched in its holt. As he led Socks up the narrow trail toward the clearing, he could see naked-assed children running about the house, shouting and throwing pebbles and generally behaving like the tribe of barbarians Mattie Bennett thought his own well-behaved son belonged to.

He paused when he cleared the last of the brush and hailed the house. It didn't do to go tramping up to a Tolliver farm, for the narrow-headed men were quick to prime their rifles, and more than one circuit rider or ped-dler had had to duck his lead. It was well known in this part of the Missouri country that you yelled before you came into the open.

The dark oblong that was the door filled with a lanky shape, which held a rifle in a bony hand. As Cleve ad-vanced the rifle rose slowly, without undue emphasis, but he knew he was covered.

Those sharp-eyed hunters could hit a bird in the eye at long range. This close, he'd be dead if he made a single threatening move. As he stepped forward, with Socks whickering softly at his back, he kept his gaze fixed on the still figure in the doorway. The children had disappeared as if they never existed, and he wondered if they had gone to earth in the bushes surrounding the bare yard.

"Mr. Tolliver?" he called. "I'd like to see Mr. Rance.

Does he still live here, or has he moved in with some of his kin farther along the creek?"

The man stepped out onto the rough-hewn board of the porch and leaned the rifle against the wall, near at hand but not quite so threatening. "Grandpa's moved down yonder with Pearlie May and her man. A step along the creek, but not too fur. Since Grandma died, he didn't seem too peart biding here."

He was not as young as his thin shape had suggested. This one of the clan was middle-aged, his neck deeply scored by weather and sun, his eyes faded. He peered at Cleve. "We know you?"

"Not since I was a boy. I've come to see Mr. Rance, so I'd better move along. Thank you kindly." Cleve stepped around the gelding and started back down the path.

As he moved he saw that four dogs had been watching from the wood, and he knew that if he had posed any threat, he would have been attacked without warning from an unexpected quarter. That was something to remember when he approached the next Tolliver dwelling.

The afternoon passed as he followed the path worn along the creekbank by human and animal feet. It was obvious that this was the main route connecting the homes of the far-flung family, and when he came to the first path diverging from the main one, he followed it through forest that showed signs of recent woodcutting.

This house was somewhat newer than the first. That one was the original one built by Rance Tolliver when he came to this country, Cleve had been told when first he visited here with his father. These logs had not turned that mossy shade of black, and the stone of the chimney, while

smoked dark, was not yet sooty with tens of years of accu-
mulation.

"Hooooayyy!" Cleve called. "Anybody to home?"

He went forward a bit farther and saw that this yard
was patched with beds of bright fall flowers, somewhat
parched but showing that a female hand was at work here.
Two ragged children, perhaps two and four, crouched in
the dust over a worn-looking terrapin.

They looked up, their pale eyes wary, and the creature
took the opportunity to take off at top speed for the nearest patch of weeds beyond the yard. Neither of the tow-
heads noticed its escape.

"Is your mother named Pearlie May?" Cleve asked the
older, who had stood and was peeing down his own leg
while sucking a grimy thumb.

"Umm-hmmn," came the affirmative, from around the
embedded thumb.

"Is your grampa Rance—but he'd be your great-
grampa, I guess—living here with you?" Cleve was glancing from the corner of his eye to spot any dog waiting for
a chance at his legs.

The boy nodded, took his thumb from his brown-circled
mouth, and yelled, *"Maaaaa!"* like a weanling calf. "Man's
hyer!"

Cleve tied Socks to a sapling beside the path and moved
slowly toward the porch, which slanted rakishly from right
to left, its steps left half-orphaned in the middle. Before he
was well into the yard, there was a quick swish of motion,
and a young woman in faded calico came onto the porch
and stared at him.

She stood without speaking, looking him up and down
as if he were a horse she was about to buy. "Who're you?"

Her voice was thin and high, and he could hear the tension.

"My name's Cleve. I need to talk to your granddaddy Rance, if he's here. It's pretty important." He watched her closely.

She flinched back, stopped, then moved forward, stepping high to avoid tripping on the out-of-line first step. She hopped down the rest of the way and approached him, her nostrils widening like those of a fox sniffing for danger. Her eyes, cornflower blue and intent, seemed to penetrate his skin and look inside at his intentions. What she saw seemed to reassure her, however.

"He's home. Takin' a nap right now. Set and rest, and I'll get you a drink of cool water, if you want. He never sleeps for long."

Cleve thanked her and sat on the edge of the porch, where the two children joined him at once, sitting at some distance but gradually edging their way closer as they sized him up. Once he had the hollowed gourd of well water in hand, the woman went back in the house, and he turned to the children.

Three mangy hounds came out from under the house and sat looking up at him. In the side yard, a scrabble of chickens pecked and quarreled softly.

"What are your names?" Cleve asked the older boy. To his surprise, it was the two-year-old who answered.

"I'm Jeffy; he's Walt. We *ain't* brothers! We're cousins."

The words were too clearly formed. This child had to be older than two, and Cleve asked, "How old are you, Jeffy?"

"I'm most four. I got took by the Injuns, and it stunted my growth, Aunt Pearlie says. They kep' me over a year.

Then they give me back and brung a batch of skins with me, to get my folks to take me." He looked proud of the fact. "I give 'em a fit, I tell you."

Cleve felt his gut clench. The boy didn't know how close he'd come to being knocked in the head as a nuisance, he knew, though he wouldn't have understood that before taking off for the wild country.

He wondered who among the tribe that took this tow-headed youngster had been soft enough to bring him back. Unless, of course, that was considered sweet revenge against the Tollivers for some past injury.

One of the dogs glanced aside at Jeffy and rose nimbly to his feet, backing away. What he had seen in the child's eyes Cleve never knew, but in a single moment the dog was a blur of motion, heading toward the woods, and the boy was after him like a streak, yelling to rival any Comanche or mountain man Cleve had ever heard vent his feelings at full cry.

The remaining dogs looked at each other, sighed with relief, and crept under the porch. He could hear the occasional dry thump of a wagging tail against wood.

Then there came a fit of deep coughing, the sound of spitting, and a gruff, "Pearl! Pearl! Where's my whiskey?"

The woman's thin voice replied, and after a while there was a shaking of the porch as a hugely heavy old man moved gingerly onto the leaning floor and looked down at his visitor. "So you want to see me? I'm right hyer. What kin I do for you?"

Cleve rose and helped the old man to a seat in the hickory rocker, whose bottom was exactly fitted to the broad fundament now settled into it. "I'm Cleve Bennett," he said.

"Jase Bennett's boy? I 'member you from away back. Used to come tradin' seed corn with your pa when you wasn't much bigger than them limbs of Satan out there tormentin' one of the dogs." Rance leaned forward and spat into the dirt.

"I've come about something really important, Mr. Rance," Cleve said. He leaned over the chair, gripping Tolliver's shoulder. "We've got problems with the boys."

Since he could remember, the Tolliver men, no matter what their ages, had been grouped together as "the boys." He was wondering right now if their being relegated to permanent childhood might not be the reason they were so erratic and dangerous to their neighbors. Now that the country was filling up, it wasn't going to be as easy for them to get away with their shenanigans as in the past.

Rance Tolliver heaved himself upright in the chair, his pale eyes widening. "What they been up to now?" he asked. His gnarled hands grasped the arms of the rocker and he accepted Cleve's help in standing.

"First, Carter shot my boy. Lije was with him. They were goin' to finish the job when my sister-in-law pulled a gun and stopped 'em. We turned those two over to the nearest marshal and then I headed for home with my son." He cleared his throat, trying to keep the tension out of his voice.

"Deke and Jim came after us and burned the prairie, trying to get us. And now a bunch of the boys are headed back to get my folks, down there on the farm. I know it as well as if I was with them."

"How old's your boy?" Rance asked, "You can't be more than twenty-two or three. He's a little feller?"

"Coming on seven," Cleve said. "He's leading his ma

and his uncle back to see if they can stop any trouble while I came up here to see if you'd go and call in your boys."

"I don't hold with shootin' young'uns." The old man sighed. "And them boys just don't understand that. They're out of hand, Cleve Bennett. This country ain't like it was, and they don't seem to understand you can't go 'round shootin' folks just 'cause you don't like the cut of their coats."

He drew a deep breath, but still his bellow startled Cleve when it came. "You, Walt! Go out in the patch and ketch old Iron Butt for me. I'm going' on a little trip."

Pearlie May came out of the house, wiping her hands on her skirt. "Grampa, you can't go noplace. You been sick, remember? You'd best stay put till Harlan comes in from the field this evening."

"Harlan can't wipe dogshit off his shoes with both hands," Rance grunted. "Them boys won't listen to nobody but me, and you know it. We're goin'."

The larger child appeared around the corner of the cabin, leading the biggest horse Cleve had ever seen. Looking at the bulk of Rance Tolliver and then at the great barrel and stocky legs of his mount, he understood just why the beast was named Iron Butt. It took that sort of strength to carry such a weight.

Cleve saddled the animal, making the trip out to the shed where the saddle was stored, over Rance's protests that he could, by God, saddle his own horse. But when the task was done, the old man mounted off the porch, being unable to hoist his bulk so high unaided.

"Now head out," Tolliver said, once he was seated on his giant steed. "If I know them boys, they're raisin' merry hell down there on the Little Sac."

Cleve whistled, and Socks, with a deft motion of his head, unlooped his rein from the sapling and came trotting smartly to the house. The children looked amazed, as well they should. They probably had never seen anything obey an order in all their short lives.

He thought about the pair as he led the way through the woods toward his goal. Was he about to kill an uncle or a cousin of theirs? And would these two grow up to be as arrogant and destructive as their kinsmen?

He sighed, ducked under a low branch, and headed off south and east toward home, hoping he and his mediator would get there in time.

chapter

— 22 —

Jase sat on the porch in his hickory splint chair, trying to look westward but prevented by the thick growth of trees and shrubs along the road. Futile tears trickled down his tracked face, and he brushed them away with his frail hands, thinking of all the things he could have done differently.

In the years since his son's first departure, amid blood and fear and anguish, Jase Bennett had learned many things he had never suspected in his life as a whole man. His father had always laid heavy hands, as well as whips and plow lines, upon his sons and his wife, and no one had ever objected.

God put the man at the head of his family, and even if the patriarch decided to kill his children or his woman, that was his heaven-sent right, according to all Jase had learned from his forebears. Nobody he knew had ever questioned that.

Not until his own flesh suffered the pain and humiliation of this kind of treatment had Jase understood what it was he had done to his wife and his sons. Years of speechlessness had made him think about his life, and guilt crept up on him until it lay thick and black over all his memories of Cleve, who had worked so hard and suffered so much at his hands.

When Cleve returned, bronzed and powerful, with a son of his own, his father knew that his awkward and difficult prayers had been answered. He had been given a second chance to learn to know his lost son.

Mattie's reaction to their only grandson astonished him, even as well as Jase understood her prejudices. She had been as patient with him, over the helpless times, as it was possible for such an impatient woman to be. Her subtle punishments along the way he accepted as well deserved, for she had known a harsh and painful life with him.

But her instant reaction against this dark-skinned boy was a physical pain to Jase, once he knew the child. Billy Wolf was quiet, disciplined, skilled at many things far beyond his age, according to a white man's way of thinking. He was a grandson to be proud of, whatever the other side of his heritage might be.

The tight knot beneath Jase's heart, which had not loosened since Cleve left home, began to uncurl. When the crippled man found the chance to make things right with his son, he felt that perhaps his last days would be happier than any that had gone before.

But, to his dismay, Mattie remained obstinately resistant to their grandchild. Cleve, as Jase had reluctantly suggested, made up his mind to leave far sooner than he would have done otherwise.

When the boy was shot, Mattie's iron will softened just a bit, but even then it was only enough to tend the boy and to make sure the travelers took along enought healing medicines to keep him from becoming ill. She had shed no tears when their son rode away beside his boy, though he suspected her racket in the kitchen afterward was intended to cover her pain at Cleve's going.

Tim, coming around the house from the back lot where he had been tending the cows, almost caught him crying. Jase couldn't have that—the boy had too many burdens as it was.

He tried to smile at his son. "Looks as if it's goin' to be a dry fall," he tried to say as Tim sank onto the step and fanned himself with his hat.

His son, who had learned to interpret his mumbled speech, nodded. "The river's just about dry except in the deep holes. I been checking every day to make sure the cattle have enough water. We may have to drive 'em up into the woods where the deep spring is, if the river gets much further down."

Tim sighed and stretched out his long legs. "I sure wish Cleve had stayed longer. We could've used his help. But I know why he left, and in his place I'd leave, too. Mama can be a hard woman sometimes."

Jase would, under other circumstances, have frowned at such disrespectful words. Now she had driven away their son, and he had no defense left for her. The worst part was, she was a good woman, hardworking and faithful.

"You reckon Cleve and the boy have got back to the tribe yet?" Tim asked, leaning forward as if he could see through trees and hills and across the intervening miles of plain. "But I guess not. He said it's a long way and takes a whet of time to make the trip. He has to go even slower because of the boy being hurt."

Mattie came to the door and said, "Supper's ready." Her mouth, thin-lipped with impatience, snapped the words as if she resented them, and Jase wondered once again if Tim would ever find a girl who could live in the same house as his folks. He was a burden and Mattie would be a terror for another woman to live with.

He struggled to his feet with the help of his youngest and hobbled into the wide kitchen, where a generous supper waited. But somehow the food, though it smelled wonderful, tasted like ashes, and he shook his head when Mattie offered seconds.

Jase had a bad feeling. He wondered if something had happened to his son, out on the plains, vulnerable to who-knows-what. Or was some danger nearer at hand? He shrugged and sighed, and his youngest came to help him to bed.

Usually the cripple slept heavily, and the nights passed as if they had never been there at all. This night, however, Jase lay awake in the big bed he shared with Mattie, though it had been years since either had moved toward the other, even to share warmth in winter. Her heavy breaths punctuated the zinging music of crickets and the shrill songs of tree frogs.

And then that racket stopped, as if someone had signaled it to halt. Jase had moved into Missouri when it was still wilderness, and he knew at once what he was hearing. Someone was sneaking up on his house.

There was no sound of voices or thud of hooves in dust, so whoever came was creeping up on the Bennett farm. For no good purpose, Jase knew, and he thought suddenly of the Tollivers who had shot his grandson. Feuds began frequently over lesser matters.

Jase struggled painfully toward his wife, who seemed very far away on her edge of the cornshuck mattress. At last he managed to nudge her in the back with an unsteady hand, patting her urgently until she moaned and turned on her other side.

"Mah! Mah!" he grunted, trying to wake her. "Uh! Uh!"

She opened her eyes. He could see her eyeballs gleam in the faint moonlight. "Jase? What on earth do you want?"

He waved his hand frantically, motioning toward the window and the silence of the night. At last she understood, for a Missouri night in summer is alive with creaks and calls. Now, except for the distant bark of a fox in the woods, it was entirely too quiet.

She rose at once, her white nightgown billowing as she hurried from the room to wake Tim. She lit no lamp, and he was pleased that she remembered how to deal with unexpected danger. In the old days it would have been Indians.

Her steps pattered softly down the hall, and Jase strained his ears to hear his son's inquiring grunt. Then two sets of feet moved swiftly to secure shutters over the windows, bars over the two thick doors, which he had built to stand off Indian attacks in their early days on the Little Sac.

She flitted into their room again and reached outside to pull the thick oak shutters across their single window. The bar thudded down, and as if in echo, a rifle boomed outside. The ball thunked solidly into the shutter, and Jase closed his eyes.

He had been right. They were under attack, and he'd bet what was left of his life, worthless as that was, that it was the Tollivers who were out there in the night, intent on vengeance.

Here he lay, useless as a log or a rock, unable to defend his own property and family from their attackers. He could only be glad that Gene and his family were safely at a distance—and then he had a terrible thought. There were dozens of Tollivers, who had taken up their land back when this country belonged to the French king. They had been breeding more of their kind ever since, prolific as rabbits.

There were enough of the ignorant bastards to circle both places and kill every Bennett here. And his son Cleve would never know. Jase wriggled his legs over the edge of the bed until they fell heavily to the puncheon floor. That gave him leverage, and he managed to sit, then to stand, his nightshirt falling about his skinny legs.

His long gun stood in the corner where it had been for twenty years. He shuffled forward and felt in the darkness for its familiar shape. The powder was kept there, too, dry in its horn, and a bag of rifle balls hung on a peg beside it. This country had never become so safe that you could leave yourself unarmed.

He cursed his feeble hands as he loaded the weapon, rammed home ball and patch, and then used the gun as a walking stick as he struggled down the hall and into the kitchen. He'd prime the pan there and wait for further developments.

Jase Bennett would fight for his home, whether it was possible or not. And if he died, then that was a damn good thing!

chapter
— 23 —

Cleve had given precise directions for taking the shortest route toward the Bennett farm. Second Son watched with pride as her son located each landmark, passed on the correct side, and moved on to the place where his kinsmen lived.

Though a few of her own kin had dismissed this "wife" of hers as a weak white man, once Yellow Hair learned the necessary skills he had proven himself time and again to be the equal of any Tsistsistas. His son was going to be as strong and wise as his father, she knew.

They passed the uprooted tangle left by some past tornado and bore to the south and east, winding among the wooded hills. When they reached a lightning-struck tree on the bank of the Little Sac, it was late afternoon.

Billy Wolf, obviously recognizing the game trail he had followed with his father, raised his hand to show that this was familiar ground. The three set off single file along the stream, which was now shallow with late summer.

The sound of hooves plopping into the water was blanketed by the kazooing of locusts in the overhanging trees. In time they rode out of the river bottom, for it veered away from the most direct route to their goal.

It was no short journey to the Bennett lodge, Billy Wolf told her when she asked. "We went for almost a day after we got here," he said. "I think we'd better go through the trees when we get near, tomorrow. If those men are there, we don't want to bump into any of them."

It was her own thought exactly, allowing for scouting out the situation before thrusting their heads into any bear cave. She nodded, but the boy dropped back.

"You would lead best now," he said. "I haven't any practice at war yet."

Lightning chuckled, a gruff *ho!* of mirth. "You have made a man of the Tsistsistas," he said to his "uncle." "This will be a warrior and a leader when he grows older."

Second Son kicked young Shadow into motion and passed Blaze, leaving Lightning's sorrel to bring up the rear. "Tell me when we are getting near," she said softly to her son, "so I will know when to veer off the path. I do not know this forest, and I do not know these people."

Then they rode in silence, listening intently to the bird-calls, the sound of shallow waters running, the swish of the breeze in the treetops, and the added voices of katydids as the day lengthened. Nothing disturbed them, and they camped that night in a dell some distance from the path, concealed from any chance traveler. Before dawn they were on their way again.

They moved more slowly, for the forest was thick, the ground uneven with unexpected hollows from which brooks sprang out of rocky ledges and ran away down toward the bigger stream. It was nearly night before they were halted by Billy Wolf.

"The track makes a bend here to follow the river. If we cross the trail now, we can cut off a good distance. I know how to go over the pastures where their animals graze so we can come up at the back of the house where the grandfather lives."

"We will go that way," she said, making her decision with her usual speed. "It will allow us to see if there are any unknown people there before we make ourselves known."

Lightning looked up through the sheltering branches into the clear sky, only just touched with light from the moon. "I will go along beside the road afoot, very softly and hidden among the trees, to see if anyone keeps watch there," he said.

Billy Wolf caught his breath. "I must be with you when you go to the house," he said, his voice thin with urgency. "My grandmother does not like people of our kind, and she will shoot you."

Again Lightning chuckled. "I am no rabbit warrior. Those who have battled with me have not known I was at hand until it was too late to kill me. Care for yourself, son of my uncle." Then the sorrel was riderless, and a dark shadow slid away along the nearby road.

Second Son dismounted and started through the trees, leading the horses and taking care not to make noise as she followed the edge of the river, for now it looped back again, and her son said this stretch lay along the pastureland of his kinsmen.

The horses crushed branches and twigs under their hooves. Around them deer darted away in panic, and she hoped anyone listening to the night would think that something was abroad, hunting for its supper. Even white men could learn the caution of her kind, she had found in her years of associating with mountain men at Rendezvous. She intended to take no risks of being detected.

There came the softest of twitters from the distant road, pitched so as to carry just so far and no farther. Lightning had sighted a watcher along the way.

Billy Wolf turned his head, a thin line of moonlight catching the gleam of his eyes. "White men almost always move along paths," he whispered. "They won't think of looking out in the woods for someone coming."

She agreed. They kept going, and after a time there was the slightest whisper of leaf on leaf and Lightning was there again.

"There are no watchers anyplace except near the path. We may go, if Wolf leads us, up to the very back of the lodge, I think, without being seen."

As his words ended, the sound of a shot blasted through the night. It was the deep roar of a rifle, and now Second Son recognized that distinctive sound as she would not have done a few years in the past when she was unfamiliar with the weapons of the trappers.

She loosed the thong holding Shadow and the sorrel

and turned to lift Billy Wolf onto Blaze. She put the lines into his hands.

"We will go down into the river now. Lead us until you can point the way to the house. Then you will remain here in the shelter of the bluff." She knew that would rankle, but she also knew he would obey.

He nodded, and she set off at a jog after the horse as it splashed rapidly along in the shallow water. When Billy Wolf pointed up a deep-cut track leading down from the pasture, Second Son could smell the acrid stink of cow manure, not very different from the smell of buffalo dung. Without looking, she thought she might follow her nose to the house.

Lightning flowed up the track, his dark skin melding with the dark soil. She turned and checked to see that her son was in place; his small body was hunched; dejected but obedient on the back of the big horse.

Then she ran toward the invisible lodge, where the occasional sound of a shot or a shout had stilled the voices of birds and night creatures. When they came within eyeshot of the dark shape that was the dwelling, both were flat on their bellies, crawling with that incredible speed they had learned back in the plains country.

They paused in the shelter of a low hedge behind the house. She could see shadows move beyond the house and in the space to the sides, though no one seemed to have set a guard at the back. There was no doorway there that she could see, and only a single window, tightly shuttered.

She gestured to the left, and her nephew slithered away, his movements too subtle to make more sound than wind in grass. Without waiting, she moved to the right, following the thick growth of flowering bushes that surrounded the pale patch of bare earth that edged the walls.

A crackle of twigs warned her that someone was ahead, and she paused to examine the area she could see in the spotted moonlight that filtered beneath the hedge. There was a dark bulk pushed back into the cover she followed.

She made out the long black shape of his gun. The head, wearing a wide-brimmed hat, was turned toward the house, and even as she watched, the rifle rose, the flint sparked, the weapon roared, and the ball resounded against the wood that closed the window on that side.

The rifle came down, and she heard noises of reloading. While he was occupied she moved, silent as a snake, behind him and cut his throat. Not even a gurgle warned his companions that they had lost one of their own.

Taking his place, Second Son checked her bowstring and nocked an arrow. When a movement caught her eye as someone dashed through a patch of moonlight in front of the house, her shaft caught him in the side.

He whirled, his cry a mixture of astonishment and pain, and went down. She shrank back deeper into her shelter, listening for any reaction from his companions.

"Gid? Gideon? You all right? What happened?" someone asked in a harsh whisper.

"I been shot. With a damned *arrow!*" came the reply. "You s'pose that renegade done brought *Injuns* here?" There was the sound of movement in the grass as the dark shape caterpillared toward the shelter of the big tree nearest it and disappeared behind it.

Second Son lay flat and slid under the low shrubbery, taking pains not to move the branches and reveal her presence. She didn't pause when someone called, "Jared! Jared! You see anything over there?"

They would be trying to rouse their dead companion, and she wanted to be far from that spot when they realized he was past replying to them. She came to a corner, and beyond it she could see the glimmer of pale dust in the moonlight. The road. She must take care not to be silhouetted against it.

She heard a hushed exclamation. Someone had found the dead Jared.

"His damn throat's been cut!" the searcher yelled. "Somebody's out here with us, Saul! How'd they git out of the place? We was watchin' both doors!"

A deep voice answered from the shadows. "They didn't git out. Somebody come up on us. Take cover, you idjits."

Second Son heard a scrambling as the two took their leader's advice. Then the deep voice boomed, "Keep low and watch out. Get out into the road again, if you can without gettin' killed. We got to join forces so nobody can slip up on us."

She lay still in the flickering shadows of the bushes, her cheek flat to the crinkly mat of fallen leaves, her gaze noting every figure that moved toward the road. A hand of men, two more, and another straggled with more noise than was seemly to gather in a dark clump beyond the gate.

A flash and a roar pursued them out of the Bennett yard; answering fire rattled against the stout logs of the house. But she heard no sound that indicated a hit. With the enemy gathered in one spot, easily watched in case they tried some strategy against those inside, there was no need to do anything at all except wait. Cleve had said to do as little damage to these Tollivers as possible, and she was content to let the rest of them live—for now.

The moon rode up the sky, and the dark gathering in the road became more distinct. Occasionally one would fire a shot at the house, but now those inside knew, it was clear, that this was only for effect, and they wasted no more ammunition.

Then Second Son felt beneath her body the vibration of hooves on earth. Riders were coming at a gallop.

She did not move. If this was Cleve and the grandfather of the Tollivers, it was good. If not—she would cope.

chapter

— 24 —

Cleve heard the distant blast of shots as he led Rance
Tolliver at a gallop across the ford at the river and onto
the road above the farm. Old Iron Butt seemed shod with
lead, so heavy was the thud of his hooves behind him;
Socks picked up his heels, seeming anxious to stay ahead
of the big horse.

Cleve didn't try to hold in the gelding. He was more
than anxious to arrive and learn what had happened to his
family. Both families.

He found that his bitterness at his mother's prejudices
leached away as he hurried toward her home. She was a

woman of the times and the place. It wasn't her fault that those who taught her hadn't known the truth that he had learned with so much difficulty and danger.

"We 'bout there?" yelled Tolliver. "My butt's about wore through and welded to this critter's backbone!"

It was clear the old man had done little riding or walking or anything but sitting for a long time now; Cleve slowed and waited for Iron Butt to come alongside.

"It's about another half mile. We better make some kind of plan so they won't shoot us before they know who we are. They're not shootin' a lot, but it doesn't sound good."

"We go right along this track, eh? No way to get off the trail?" Rance asked.

"Ahuh."

"Then let me lead the way. I know them boys better'n anybody alive, and I can call 'em to heel like a pack of coon hounds. You fall back a little so they won't know right away that you're here. Then when I get 'em corralled, you can come up with me. Once I get my bluff in on 'em, they settle down pretty quick."

Cleve followed the huge horse, watching the solid shape of the rider joggle in and out of the moonlight sifting through overhanging branches. "Your bluff? I thought you ran those boys from teeth to tail," he said.

There came a muffled laugh. "I couldn't whup a sick kitten, boy. I'm too old and wore out and sick even to make a ride like this'n." Indeed, his gruff voice had weakened noticeably.

"Once you get me down from here, you're goin' to have to drag me to a bed or a pile of leaves and let me lay till I can move again. But them boys don't know that, and don't you tell 'em, for God's sake."

That gave Cleve something else to worry about as they moved quickly along the road and into sight of the stretch before his mother's front gate. Then he forgot to worry about Rance Tolliver.

A cluster of tall, lanky men lay in the shadow of the hedge of rose vines and crepe myrtles, only semivisible in the mottled shade of the trees. Even as he watched, one raised a rifle and fired at the house beyond the hedge and fence. There was no return fire.

Before the shooter could reload, Rance bellowed, "You, Jim Conyers! Hold yer fire, damn you!"

There was a convulsed movement among the blur of bodies and limbs, which quickly sorted themselves out into eight men. They stood, without thought of being shot from the house, brought up instantly by the patriarch's words.

Cleve had one moment to hope desperately that his wife, nephew, and son would not show themselves once the hostilities were ended. He didn't need any more anti-Indian emotions roused in these hot-tempered people. Then he knew, without any doubt, that Second Son would judge the situation wisely and behave accordingly.

He heard, with his plains-trained ear, a subtle crickle of sound. Not Second Son—there would have been no sound at all from her. Maybe one of his family was out and about.

"Tim?" he asked. "You there?"

His brother did not step out into the moonlight, but he grunted an affirmative. Cleve grinned for the first time since leaving his people and heading for Horse Creek.

"You boys just left your horses to ramble?" came the

question from Rance Tolliver, "or did you picket 'em proper?"

The one he'd called Jim ducked his head, cleared his throat, and said, "We tied the critters back in the woods. They're all right, Grampa. We ain't dumb, you know."

"I *don't* know! Takes eight of you to come down here and tackle a crippled old man, a old lady, and the only son they got left at home, does it? And even if you'd gone to t'other house, there's nothin' there but another man, a woman, and two little bitty girls. Mighty brave boys we got! I could spit on you all!"

Cleve would not have believed, if anyone had told him the tale, that eight grown men ranging in age from twenty to fifty could change so quickly. Instead of being mighty warriors, intent on rousting out those in the cabin, they bore themselves like newly spanked children.

Their heads drooped. Their eyes, cast downward, examined the ground at their feet. A more sheepish bunch he had never seen in all his life. A voice muttered from the middle of the bunch, "There was nine. Somebody cut Jared's throat. You mean you want us to let off of a blood feud?"

Rance didn't let up a bit. "If Jared hadn't been where he oughtn't to be, nothin' would have happened to him. You git home, you hear me? There's not a one of you that's worth killin', anyway."

From the forest beyond the yard fence there came the soft twitter of a disturbed night bird. Not one of those gathered before his old home took any note of it. But to Cleve it said that Second Son was at hand, hidden but ready for anything he might need.

A whippoorwill fluttered its cry from the other side of

the house. That would be Lightning. His son, he knew, would be concealed with the horses, someplace safe.

"Now git that body on a horse and move yourselves to home!" the old man boomed. "I don't want to find a man of you outside his own house till I say he can go. Move!"

"You want to come in and rest?" Cleve asked Rance Tolliver. "I know you've got to be just about tuckered out."

The old man sighed. "That would be plumb welcome, Mr. Bennett. You think your folks would mind puttin' me up till I can ride back home again?"

Conyers turned back and glared at the old man. "You don't mean you're *misterin'* this bastard and intend to stay with his Injun-lovin' folks?" he asked, his voice harsh with fury.

Rance Tolliver glared back, and under the fury of his moonlit gaze the man lowered his head and stared at the ground. "I *mister* people that deserve it by actin' like grown men. *Boys* go off half-cocked and shoot young'uns. *Boys* go railin' into the woods after folks that can't defend themselves. *Boys* set fire to the grasslands when they go hightailin' after somebody that protected his son from 'em." He drew a deep breath and let it out with great control and precision.

The group of men moved away fast, dreading what might follow. Cleve kept himself from laughing with difficulty, but he knew better than to interfere with the old man's handling of his kin. He understood what he was doing, and he was measuring to the inch just what it would take to get his unruly sons and grandsons back to Horse Creek.

Those few who still stood in the road holding guns were

now aiming them at the pale dust of the road. Tim stepped out of the gate, a shadow in the tenuous light, and began taking them from those Tolliver men who were still subjected to the flail of their patriarch's tongue.

Cleve realized that they were not entirely conscious of the transaction, so cowed were they by the old man's eloquent and biblical phrases. He could hear the clatter of hooves as the others brought horses to their trapped kinsmen.

The last rifle was collected and handed to someone inside the shadows of the hedge. Ma, Cleve knew, would be there at hand when needed. But to his surprise the big shadow that appeared in the gap was that of his father, who was shuffling carefully forward, his own rifle cradled in the crook of his better arm.

Cleve dropped from Socks's back and moved quietly toward Jase, keeping clear of the subdued group still listening to Rance's tirade. He touched Tim's shoulder as he passed. When he faced his father, he stopped and looked into those moon-silvered eyes.

Jase tried to smile, the droop in one side of his face spoiling the effect. "Baw?" he asked urgently. "Arrigh'?"

Cleve understood as if he had spoken perfectly clearly. "Billy Wolf is fine. He led my people back here to help you, if you needed it," he said, pitching his voice so low that only the two beside him could hear. "They left him someplace safe, I know. Here, let me help you back inside, Pa."

"I'll help the old codger yonder when he finishes," Tim said. "You and Pa go ahead. Ma's back there having conniptions because Pa just came right on out as if he was himself again. You want to call in the boy now?"

Cleve murmured, "It's best that these Tollivers don't ever know that my people came back with me. Rance has 'em in hand now, and he'll send them back to Horse Creek with their tails between their legs, if I know the signs. Then I'll signal for my family to come."

Jase moved more surely than he had before, stepping, with only minor halting, toward his own porch. Cleve had to lift him up the steps, but after that he seemed fairly steady.

Mattie was clucking and worrying about him. "Old fool, just runs out like he was a twenty-year-old. Hasn't held that rifle since you left, Cleve, and here he is with it loaded and primed." She peered into the pan and sniffed. "What's left of the priming after he staggers all over kingdom come with it."

She hustled Jase into the house and settled him in his big chair. The kettle on the stove was beginning to steam, and it was obvious she had built up the fire even more and intended to offer refreshment to anyone who came, whether he wanted it or not.

The raw tang of corn whiskey came to Cleve's nostrils, and he knew that their visitor would, indeed, want to indulge in Mattie Bennett's peppermint tea that she would certainly fortify with some of Gene's homemade whiskey. He wouldn't refuse it himself, for his hard ride had left him tired to the bone.

After a time Tim came into the kitchen carrying Rance Tolliver's bundle and his rifle. Behind him, the giant stumped heavily over the scrubbed flooring and sank into one of the stout handmade chairs with much creaking of wood and groaning of aged flesh.

"We're much obliged to you for coming," said Mattie.

She handed him a cup, which he sniffed and then drained with one gulp. Refilling it, she continued, "We had no intention of getting into any sort of squabble with our neighbors, you know. Our son hasn't been home for years now, and he brought his own son to meet his grandparents. Surely you can see this wasn't meant to start any feud."

Rance sighed and leaned back in the chair. "Madame," he said, in tones unlike his usual uncouth twang, "if I hadn't understood that, I wouldn't be cluttering up your house right now. No kin of mine shoots a child and gets away unscathed. To me a child is precious."

Cleve, in turn, sighed. It was a surprising world. People you thought were ignorant and lacking in wit turned out to be smarter and kinder than you might think. People who seemed cruel and despicable, like his father, turned out to be kindly, given the right circumstances. People who had seemed all-knowing and without flaw proved to have weaknesses like his mother's prejudice against his son.

"Nothing much is the way you think it is," he said aloud.

Jase turned bright eyes toward him and nodded vigorously. Mattie looked puzzled. Only the old man seemed undisturbed.

"Call in your people," he said. "It's time I met this son of yours, and your other family. I never met any of the wild warriors of the plains before. It's time I did, before my turn comes to die."

Cleve rose and stepped to the door. He sent the call of a hunting hawk into the night. It was not the correct hour for such a cry, and that would tell his waiting family that it was time to meet this group they had come so far to protect.

Out of the night came three whistles, two near, one distant but distinct. They were there, and soon they would arrive, his son, his wife, and his nephew. Pride filled him as he waited for them to come.

chapter

— 25 —

Waked from a sound sleep, exhausted from working extra hard to conceal from herself her grief at her son's leaving, Mattie had required a moment to understand that her home was under attack. Then she moved automatically to secure her defenses.

The fact that Jase was up and about didn't really get through to her for some time. Only when he came shuffling into the dark kitchen and the faint flicker from the coals she had uncovered in the fireplace glinted on his rifle did she realize what he was doing.

"You're not able to do that! Jase, put it back before you

shoot somebody!" she objected. But he didn't. He ignored her as if she hadn't spoken.

Then she was busy with her own rifle, trying to see through the loopholes bored in the thick oak shutter, in order to find a target. It wasn't the first time she had helped to defend her home, over the years, but she found that she was getting too old for this sort of thing. It was time people left her in peace.

For a short while rifle balls rattled against the thick walls, and once a random shot hit a chink in a shutter and crossed the room to thud into the log wall there. She ignored it. If you worried about getting shot, you might as well crawl in a hole and die right off. She hadn't lived as long as she had by letting herself be scared away from doing the right thing.

The thick overhang of trees around the house cast shadows that made it impossible to see the attackers, who remained motionless and under cover. From time to time someone would dart through a milky patch of moonlight, and she or Tim or Jase would send a rifle ball after him, but she thought they hit no one. It was just too dark to see.

The night wore on and the firing thinned to an occasional shot, mostly to keep her family inside, she was sure. When it seemed safe, she stuffed cloth in every crack she could find and then built up the fire in her prized iron cookstove. She was glad of its iron door, which concealed the light of the blaze from anyone who might peep through a crack in a shutter.

She always kept a bucket of water sitting in a corner, for you never knew what would happen, even in these tame days. Mattie filled her kettle and set it on the stovetop to heat. If anyone was wounded, hot water would be needed.

If not, hot tea and whiskey were always good to settle the nerves after a battle.

After getting out her already prepared bags of lint, she set herself to tearing old linen into strips for bandages. If they weren't used now, they would be put to use another time. There was never a shortage of injuries on the farm.

Between the long *r-r-r-ips* a shot still sounded, now and then, but it was obvious that the Tollivers intended to do something more aggressive to push the family out of the house. She dreaded fire more than anything, but there was little they could do about it if one was kindled in a spot they couldn't reach.

Voices called in front. "Gid! Gideon! You all right? What happened?"

Tim, close beside her, whispered, "Something's happening. He sounds scared. Who could be out there?"

"Maybe Gene. You think so?" she replied softly.

"Not Gene. He'd have whistled. No, this is somebody else, unless the Tollivers have fallen out among themselves." Tim leaned close to the shutter and peered through the gap left by the rifle ball.

"I can't see anything out there, though. In a bit, if nothing happens, I'm going to see if I can slide through the back window and check things out. We can't stay stopped up in here forever, and if they decide to try building a fire against the house, we're in big trouble." He set his gun barrel in the hole and let off a blast.

"Just to keep 'em careful," he said.

Mattie nodded, though he probably couldn't see her in the thin red streaks of light that escaped around the circular iron "eyes" of the stove. Then she raised her head, straining to hear.

"Timothy, I hear horses. I feel horses. Somebody is coming fast. Don't you hear them?"

Perhaps it was her hope or her dread that let her feel the approach of the riders, for it was some moments before her son let out a gasp. "You're right. They're getting close now. I'm going out! The Tollivers are going to be busy with whoever is out on the road."

He left her, and she followed him into the room she shared with Jase. When he pushed the shutter open and slithered over the windowsill, she checked to make sure he met no resistance. Then she secured the shutter again and went back to stand in the kitchen beside Jase, who leaned against the wall beside the door, his rifle reprimed.

Together they waited for what might come next. For the first time in decades she felt close to her husband, warmed by his presence. When he insisted on going outside at last, sliding painfully through the door she held open for him, she was reassured by one familiar voice in the road.

The lack of any fire from the Tollivers was a hopeful sign, she thought as she watched his tall shape fade into the shadows. Somebody had come and the attackers were distracted, if nothing more.

Thinking over the events of that night, later in her life, Mattie had a hard time sorting out events. First had come Cleve with Jase. Then Tim assisted Rance Tolliver, of all people, into the kitchen and settled him in a chair capable of holding his huge weight.

She had drunk more than one cup of her fortified tea, so she was surprised when Cleve whistled out the side door. When the three Indians entered her house, they blurred before her eyes for a moment before coming into focus.

There was a tall man, slender and very young, dressed in leather leggings and a loose vest of doeskin beaded with bright quills. He wore a sort of breastplate made of thin bones or quills, which rattled softly as he moved. His face was long, the features sharp and fine.

Her grandson stood beside him, erect and at ease, his dark eyes bright and alert. To her surprise the journey he had made seemed not to have made him ill.

Behind the boy there was a short, square shape, dressed similarly to the young man, except that instead of a vest he wore a sleeveless leather shirt, laced together in front. The glossy hair was held with a thong in which eight feathers were secured. A bow hung about one shoulder, and a knife rode in a sling at one hip.

This one was older than the other man, the face composed but stern, the eyes calm, assessing everything and everyone in the cramped kitchen. A man to fear, she thought at once. A man to do great deeds, if he had been white instead of copper-colored. Something about his presence held a dignity that almost scared her.

Mattie wondered who these people might be. They did not look like savages, despite their dress, but something in their bearing told her they were not subject to any law she knew. A glimmer of understanding awoke in her mind. Was this what Cleve found to admire in those wild plains people who had provided him with a wife and a son?

And then Cleve was leading the two strangers to her chair. He bent over her and took her hands in his. "Mama," he said, "this is my nephew Rakes the Sky with Lightning. And this . . . this is my wife, Second Son, warrior of the Tsistsistas. If you'll let yourself, you'll like her."

The dark face looked down at her, the eyes cool, the expression rather stern. But there was no hostility there. Rather, there was curiosity in the eyes of this woman who looked like a man.

It came as a shock, for she had taken this one for a man without question. Women didn't have such confidence or such obvious strength of mind and body. Mattie felt at a loss, for never had she dreamed of welcoming such a daughter-in-law into her family.

"She and Lightning never hesitated a minute when I told them the Tollivers might come back here and do you and Pa harm. They followed Billy Wolf this way while I went after Rance, here, and they were here in case you needed 'em to fight off an all-out attack or to put out a fire meant to smoke you out." Her son was staring down, his expression anxious.

But Mattie Bennett, whatever her personal prejudices, had never been guilty of ingratitude. She knew, meeting that dark gaze, that this woman would have gone fearlessly to her death defending the unknown people of her man. It was clear in every line of her face and her strong body.

This was no beautiful seductress, such as Mattie had conjured up in her imagination. She was a powerful and determined person. Like herself, Mattie realized with sudden recognition. Except that she had always hidden her strength to save herself from abuse.

She tried to smile, but the whiskey had made her dizzy. She held out her hand, instead.

Callused fingers gripped her own. The hand was warm, dry, as strong as her son's. "Mother of Yellow Hair," the Cheyenne said, "I see you with joy. Your son has been good to my people. He is a fine husband, though among my people he is called my wife, and he has given me a strong son."

The English was pronounced a bit strangely, the choice of words rather stilted. The voice was warm, low, with a hint of the guttural in places, but she could find no fault with what this person said.

With some difficulty, Mattie stood. "I thought I didn't want to see the woman Cleve married," she said. "I was wrong. I needed to know you, Second Son. I needed to learn what I never knew before, that your people can be perhaps a bit like ours. I'm glad you're here. I'd pour you some tea, but I've had a drop too much liquor in mine. I think I'd spill it."

Cleve laughed, his voice booming with joyous relief. "Then everything's all right!" he said. "I wasn't going to be easy until you two met, if it took ten years more. Now we can go back home to the mountains and know we left you satisfied with how things are with me."

Rance Tolliver leaned forward and looked closely at her daughter-in-law. "I wouldn't want to meet you in a stand-up fight," he said. "Even when I was a young'un. I never much taken to Indians, but I'm glad to meet you."

Second Son turned to him and looked into his eyes. "I have killed one of your people," she said. "I regret that it was necessary, but he was in my way and he was firing at the house. He was beneath the hedge, out there." She gestured toward the side yard.

Tolliver turned red. "Jared had his throat cut. That was the one, and his kin have him slung across a horse and on the way back to Horse Creek right now."

"They called for Jared," she said. "He did not answer."

Mattie felt a knot form in her stomach. Were they going to go right into another fight, this one a blood feud?

The old man sank back with a sigh. "Don't worry about it. I been tryin' to get rid of that son of a bitch since he married my granddaughter Imogene. Would have shot him myself if I'd been a bit younger and some sprier."

"I killed him quickly," said this remarkable woman, her expression unchanged. "He never knew."

Mattie felt her stomach unclench. For some reason that only God knew, Second Son had killed the one of the Tolliver bunch that the patriarch disliked. There would be no feud. Her son could go about his life with his other family without having to look behind for a pack of curs at his heels.

And he would go. She understood that as she rose, a bit unsteadily, and managed to pour out a cup of fortified tea for the newcomers to her clan. In such company, he would be as safe as it was possible to be, out there in the wild country.

Jase reached for her hand, and she squeezed his fingers. Perhaps, in her old age, she would find peace at last.

chapter

— 26 —

"I hate to go, Mama," Cleve said to Mattie Bennett, standing on her porch in a mist of rain. "Now that you've got to know my folks, I think you might get to be friends with 'em in time."

His mother crimped her mouth tight, stopping back tears, he knew. Then she said, "Mayhap it's best this way, son. I'm an old woman, and changing my ways isn't easy. Your woman is as hardheaded as I am, I can tell by looking at her. We haven't anything to talk about, because I can't understand why she'd want to be a man, and I can see she can't understand my wanting to be nothing but a woman."

"That's for sure and certain," Cleve replied. The days since his second arrival had been interesting but not particularly peaceful. Second Son did not argue or appear to notice his mother's occasional flare-ups, but she had taken some very long walks through the forest beyond the river.

"The thing I hate most is that I'm just now coming around to knowing my grandson," she said. A spark of warmth kindled in Cleve's heart as she continued: "He's a likely little fellow. If you forget his coloring, he's quite a bit like my own brother Ned that died when we were little."

There was no doubt about his father's feelings for the boy. Jase was sitting in his chair with Billy Wolf perched on his knee. The two had learned in some way to communicate without words, and they now were staring at each other. He thought they were memorizing each other's faces.

Both his brothers waited down in the yard and Sarah and the girls were out by the gate, petting the horses. Cleve hated good-byes, but he knew it was time.

"Take care of yourself, Mama," he said, lifting her in a hug, then setting her down again amid a swirl of calico.

He turned and gripped his father's hand. Then he lifted his son and dropped off the edge of the porch. His brothers were as silent as he while they finished loading the packs onto the horses and saw the group mounted.

He wondered what Lightning was thinking about this white man's way—it was far more demonstrative than the Tsistsistas ever dreamed of being.

Second Son mounted Shadow and from that height she looked over the gate at Mattie. Neither said anything, and Cleve clucked to Socks and turned up the road.

Behind him he heard his son's voice calling, "Good-bye! Good-bye!" to his cousins and other kin.

Once they were headed west, the faint sadness he had felt dissipated. They were going back home to the wide grasslands, the shining mountains, the crisp clean winds of the heights.

"We might as well spend the winter with your folks, if you'd like," he called to Second Son. "We'll be mighty late gettin' to the high country. We been working our tails off for a lot of winters now, and it's time we sat around and shot the breeze and swapped lies with Singing Wolf and Buffalo Horn and the rest of 'em. What do you say?"

She turned a beaming glance back toward him, and he knew that was what they would do.

Behind him Lightning grunted. "Yellow Hair," he said softly, "if we see Comanche along the way . . . I know it is late for raiding, but *if* we do . . . we might steal some horses. Do you think?"

The veneer of civilization that Cleve had felt enwrapping him during his visit home seemed to peel off like a used-up skin. The Cheyenne had gone to his aid without question. Why shouldn't he help them with their own project?

"I don't see why not," he said. "Besides, I've still got a grudge against those devils for taking my boy. You spot a bunch of Shinni, nephew, and we'll take every horse they've got."

They crossed the Little Sac and headed out, saving the horses but making time nevertheless. They would reach the plains in a few days, and then, Cleve felt with sudden conviction, they were destined to find a band of Comanche returning from their summer raids, fat and contented and driving all kinds of stolen mounts for his people to steal.

He laughed aloud. He felt in his gut it was going to happen, and he, by God, was going to enjoy it to the hilt.

If you enjoyed
BLOOD KIN
by John Killdeer,
be sure to look for the next novel in his
MOUNTAIN MAJESTY
series,
available soon wherever Bantam titles
are sold.

THE MAGNIFICENT NEW SAGA OF THE MEN
AND WOMEN WHO TAMED THE MOUNTAINS!

It was a land of harsh beauty and fierce dangers—
and the men and women who made their
livelihood in the Rocky Mountains had to use
every resource of strength and shrewdness to
survive there. Trapper Cleve Bennett and the
Indian woman he loves live a saga of survival
on the high frontier.

MOUNTAIN MAJESTY
BOOK 1: WILD COUNTRY
❏ 28885-7 $3.99/$4.99 in Canada
BOOK 2: THE UNTAMED
❏ 28886-5 $3.99/$4.99 in Canada
BOOK 3: WILDERNESS
RENDEZVOUS
❏ 28887-3 $4.50/$5.50 in Canada
BOOK 4: BLOOD KIN
❏ 28888-1 $4.99/$5.99 in Canada

by
John Killdeer